Andrew Shuman

The Loves of a Lawyer, his Quandary, and How it Came Out

Andrew Shuman

The Loves of a Lawyer, his Quandary, and How it Came Out

Reprint of the original, first published in 1875.

1st Edition 2024 | ISBN: 978-3-38538-818-5

Verlag (Publisher): Outlook Verlag GmbH, Zeilweg 44, 60439 Frankfurt, Deutschland
Vertretungsberechtigt (Authorized to represent): E. Roepke, Zeilweg 44, 60439 Frankfurt, Deutschland
Druck (Print): Books on Demand GmbH, In de Tarpen 42, 22848 Norderstedt, Deutschland

THE

LOVES OF A LAWYER,

HIS QUANDARY,

AND HOW IT CAME OUT.

By ANDREW SHUMAN,

EDITOR CHICAGO EVENING JOURNAL.

CHICAGO:

W. B. KEEN, COOKE & CO.

113 AND 115 STATE STREET.

1875.

The Loves of a Lawyer.

CONTENTS.

INTRODUCTORY.

INTRODUCTORY.

HE was an elderly gentleman, the Judge was, with a profusion of gray hair, as soft and smooth as silk, and a face as kindly as that of a young girl. I chanced to meet him in a railway car, we being fellow-travelers, homeward bound, on the long journey from San Francisco, eastward. We occupied adjoining seats, took pleasantly to each other, and whiled away much of the tedium of those five days, coming through the great mountains and the vast plains, in free-and-easy conversation. After almost every topic of current news, politics, literature, science and philosophy had been exhausted, we made drafts upon our funds of anecdote, and finally, as a last resort, entertained each other with incidents and experiences from our own life-history.

The Judge was one of the most sociable and entertaining men I had ever met in my life, and never will I forget the deep feeling he exhibited at certain pathetic periods when relating the following story, which he appropriately called

"MY GREAT QUANDARY."

THE BEGINNING OF IT.

THE

LOVES OF A LAWYER.

CHAPTER I.

THE BEGINNING OF IT.

WHEN I was a young man—which is many years ago—I was a boarder in a family of three. Those three were a motherly widow, her daughter and a niece, the two latter of whom were but a few years younger than I. They were good folk—cultivated, pleasing, companionable. I had but recently graduated from college, and, being homeless, chanced to make my headquarters with the good widow,

who insisted upon my calling her mother — and
certain it is that no mother could be more studi-
ous of the comfort, or more interested in the
welfare, of a son than she was in my behalf. It
was a home, indeed, and she was as motherly as
possible, and her two young ladies were as sisterly as possible. I became very fond of them.
They were my companions in the drawing-room
in the evening, and I was their inevitable escort
to parties, balls, lectures, amusements. They
had other associates in the society of the town,
and so had I, but somehow a marked preference
for each others society in time developed itself,
continued to grow, and was mutually confessed.

It wasn't *love*—I think not; at all events we
did not act as lovers do, nor did I entertain a
lover's emotions, dreams or anticipations. I was
just entering actively upon my chosen life-work
—a profession to which I devoted all the energy
and devotion of my youthful ardor and ambition; and the thought of love, courtship or marriage seldom found lodgment with me. They

called themselves my sisters, as the old lady, (not very old, either,) called herself my mother, and I felt like a brother toward the maidens. And that was the extent of my thoughts and feelings, and I never suspected that theirs partook of a more tender character.

The widow's name was Wilkins — Mrs. Jane Wilkins, the relict of Mr. Thomas Wilkins, merchant, who had been dead ten years when I became a member of her domestic circle. Her daughter's name was Frances — Miss Frances Wilkins, aged twenty-two, of quiet, reserved, and dignified demeanor;· womanly, majestic, and accomplished in all that renders a young lady attractive to a young man of elevated ideas. The niece's name was Laura — Miss Laura Ferris, an orphan, aged twenty, whose parents were suddenly snatched from her, an only child, during the last visitation of the cholera. Her father had been a man of wealth, and she inherited it. She was unlike her cousin in appearance and disposition, and yet like her in taste and refinement. Frances was sedate, Laura sprightly; Frances was a brunette, with large dark eyes and a profusion of dark brown hair, and tall and stately as a queen, while Laura had deep blue eyes, auburn curls, and was short and compact of form. Although thus unlike, yet they harmonized as companions, and had they been sisters, could not have been more devoted to each other. It was a harmonious family, and I failed to discover that my entrance into it marred its unity or disturbed its equanimity. The only effect seemed to be its enlargement from an accordant trio to a joyous quartette.

Three years had passed since I had become a member of Mrs. Wilkins' household, when, one evening, while sitting alone with her in the drawing-room, she suddenly diverted the conversation from the topic in hand to myself and my future.

"Samuel, my son," she said, in her usual motherly way, "do you realize the fact that you are approaching thirty, and will soon be classed among the old bachelors?"

"Yes, mother, yes," I replied, "I am aware of that, but who would call me an *old* bachelor? I am still a mere boy, and am just beginning to get a good start in my profession. Can't think of marrying; not yet, if ever at all."

"There you will make a great mistake," she said; "the longer you put it off, the more confirmed a bachelor you will become. A man like you should marry, by all means."

"But who would marry me?" I asked.

"Almost any good girl in the city; they all know you, and they all like you."

"I don't know about that, but I do know that I have not given a thought to the subject."

"It is time you did; let me tell you that as a friend." And then, hesitating a moment, she resumed, with much seriousness: "Do you know that either of my two girls here, whom you call sisters, would make you a most excellent wife? Have you ever thought of that?"

2

Here was a puzzler, and I instantly divined the good woman's object in opening this conversation.

"I have never thought of either of them in that connection," I replied; "they are worthy to be the wives of the greatest and best men in the world, but I am only a poor young lawyer, who has a name and a fortune yet to make. I could not ask either of them to sacrifice herself for my sake; it would be presumptuous in me to ask or expect it."

'You are all wrong, Samuel, all wrong, I assure you. Oh, I wish you knew as well as I do, how much those girls think of you! But now let me ask you one question; you may answer it or not, as you choose; all I require is frankness on your part."

"Well, certainly."

"Which of those girls do you love best?"

"Upon my word, I can't answer you that; I don't know. They are excellent young women, both of them."

"Well, now, Samuel," said she, warming up, "you must have a preference for one or the other; one who sees so much of them and knows them as well as you do, must be able to decide which is the better of the two, and which would make the better wife for you, if you were to choose between them."

"If marrying is the question, I think if I were to consider that, with a view of arriving at a decision, I would have to conclude to marry them both," I rejoined, laughing.

"Nonsense!" she exclaimed, and was about to leave the room, when a thought seemed to occur to her suddenly, and approaching my chair, she said, in a half-whisper: "Those two girls love you, Samuel, and let me tell you, in confidence, that they are about to *test* you. They have made an agreement between them to ascertain, by a process that I am not at liberty to divulge, which of them you love best. My object in telling you the secret is to warn you so that you may be prepared for the ordeal, and so that you may, if you feel so disposed, analyze your own feelings sufficiently to decide a question which, after this evening's conversation with you, I am convinced you are not now prepared for."

With that she withdrew. That which she told me made me uneasy, nervous, fearful. Love, with a view of marriage, was to me a new theme of thought; and yet the good madam's conversation and her warning of the young ladies' test-plot convinced me that her motherly interest and their sisterly regard had assumed a more serious sentiment than that of mere friendship, and that I really occupied a very delicate and trying position in this goodly household; a position for which I was not prepared; one which might cause me great embarrassment, and, what was worse, might cause those to whom I was so warmly but disinterestedly attached, disappointment and grief. The thought troubled me, and the fact that the young ladies, on that particular evening, kept their own rooms, not joining me in the drawing-room, as was their usual evening

custom, only contributed to my increasing anxiety. " Which of them *do* I love best?" I asked
myself. And the answer came: " They are dear
creatures, *both*, and if I really love them, I
esteem them both alike." And this was the
conclusion of the half-revery, half-argument,
which, while sitting there silently and alone,
occupied my mind during the remainder of the
evening, and I finally retired to lose myself and
forget my puzzling problem and its subjects in
sleep.

Next morning Frances and Laura, who at
breakfast seemed less talkative than usual, suddenly came upon me in the hall-way, as I was
about leaving for my office, the former as sedate
as usual, and the latter as sprightly as ever, and
desired me to tarry a few moments—they had a
favor to ask of me.

"I'll grant it before you ask it," I promptly
replied; "now, what is it?"

Laura was to make the speech, and she did it
bravely. "Samuel," she said, "either Frances

or I will have to go to grandmother's to stay a few months, to be company for her in her lonely home in the country; it is over an hundred miles away, you know; neither of us wants to go away from home so long, and we have agreed to ask you to decide the question which of us shall go, and to abide by your decision without a murmur."

"Why don't you draw lots? That would be a speedy method, and save me from a disagreeable responsibility, for indeed I cannot decide between you."

But they insisted, and declared that I *must* decide. "If you don't, I will never forgive you," said Laura. "If you don't," said Frances, " I will never call you brother again."

"Well, now, girls," I replied, "I object to either of you going away; I decide that both of you shall stay at home."

"No, no, that can not be," they declared, in chorus.

"If you wait for me to decide that either of

you shall go, neither of you will go; that's set-tled," I said, very firmly.

Seeing that I was in earnest, they dismissed the subject laughingly, but were evidently disappointed. They did not suspect that I had been warned of their game. As I was leaving the house, and just before closing the door behind me, I chanced to hear Frances, addressing her mother, exclaim: "It was a failure; he wouldn't decide, and we can't induce him to. We must try some other device."

IN THE LAWYER'S OFFICE.

CHAPTER II.

"SAMUEL TRAVERSE, Attorney-at-Law."
Those were the simple words that marked
my office door in Barrister's Row, in the city of
Westerly. This was my professional workshop;
here I daily busied myself in the books of the
great legal philosophers and commentators;
here I studied, labored, waited and hoped; here,
day by day, I sat and pondered and dreamed.
Occasionally a client chanced to drop in for
advice, and once in a great while even a party to
a small suit came in to engage my services as
counsel. But the first few years passed slowly
and heavily, and sometimes I seriously entertained a thought of removing from the town and

seeking a more favorable field in which to practice my profession. Here older lawyers had a
monopoly, and I would have to wait on and struggle on for years in poverty and impatience before
I could hope to accomplish anything. To an
ambitious young man, who was conscious of his
ability to cope successfully with other men in the
profession, if he could but get a fair start and
have a fair chance, this situation was becoming
discouraging, especially in view of the fact that
three years had now dragged themselves over my
head since that sign had been nailed upon my
office door, and that as yet but few clients, and
those poor, petty ones, and but little business,
and that bringing a mere pittance in the way
of fee or reward, had come to me.

"*I* fall in love? *I* think of marrying? Poor
as a beggar, and no prospect ahead; what could
I do with a wife? Absurd!" It was thus I
reasoned with myself as I sat in my office, alone,
as usual, thinking of that morning's scene with
the young ladies at Mrs. Wilkins'. "As well

think of flying into heaven bodily as to think of marrying, under present circumstances." And I dismissed the subject summarily from my mind, or at least tried to. Not an easy matter. In spite of my efforts to concentrate. my thoughts upon the pages of my law-books; the treatises on Pleadings, Practice, Evidence, and the Common Law, by the great teachers and expounders of the profession; in spite of my resolute endeavors to master certain provisions of the Code; in spite of my efforts, with the statute-books open before me, to disentangle a knotty case that a poor tenant who was being oppressed by a merciless landlord intrusted to me on the day before, he agreeing to call this afternoon to learn my advice; in spite of all resolution and circumstance, those young ladies at Mrs. Wilkins' would intrude themselves upon my thoughts, mingling their bright eyes, sweet faces and musical voices with the profound propositions of the legal commentators in the books, and with the intricate verbiage of legislative enactments on " Landlord and Tenant;" and I must confess that had the ingredients of my mentality been carefully analyzed and weighed on that day, the analyzer and weigher would have decided that there were at least three parts of Woman to one part of Law in that uncontrollable confusion of mind and that chaos of irresolution and quandary.

UNEXPECTED DEPARTURE.

CHAPTER III.

I WAS sitting alone in Mrs. Wilkins' drawing-room. It was a quiet, lovely summer evening. Presently the madam came in. "Samuel," said she, "Laura has gone to her grandmother's; left this afternoon. The girls felt very badly when you refused to decide which of them should go, and I was sorry I had warned you of their intended test of your preference. Although it was a device by which they thought to compel you unconsciously to indicate your preference for one or the other of them, yet the fact that they felt it a duty that one or the other of them should go and spend a few months with their grandmother, was no *ruse*. My girls are incapapable of deception, my son; that you know."

3

"Well, now, mother, if I had decided which of them should go, what would have been the effect as regards my supposed preference between them—would the one that was to go or the one that was to stay have been considered my favorite?"

"It is not likely," she replied, "that one would voluntarily separate himself from the one he loves, is it?"

"Ah, yes, I see. And so Laura has gone? And without bidding me good-bye?"

"Both the girls have concluded that you don't love either of them. I think they are mistaken, but that is their inference."

"They certainly are mistaken," I said, "but, for the life of me, I cannot decide that I love one more than the other. At all events, it wouldn't make any difference, for, to tell the plain truth, I cannot afford to love anybody very ardently. I am too poor to marry; I see too long and desperate a professional struggle before me to allow myself to think of such a thing."

"Two can fight a battle better than one, my son, especially the battle of life; be assured of that."

"Yes, but if both are poor as beggars?"

"In the case of either Frances or Laura, this would not be so; neither of them is either poor or in immediate danger of penury. Their fathers made ample provision for them."

"If I ever marry," I remarked, "it will not be until I shall have the means in my possession to support a wife independently of her own property. What she might have would be hers; I could not be dependent upon her wealth for our joint maintenance."

"In this you talk like a boy, my son," she said, energetically; "you may depend upon it that the woman who loves you, and is willing to join life's fortunes and destinies with yours, has nothing that she would not have you share with her; yes, not only share, but own, control and possess. What belongs to a true woman, who marries a true man, is his, with all her heart; don't doubt that."

And the madam left the room, her daughter Frances entering as she left.

"Oh, Samuel," said the young lady, taking my hand, "Laura has gone, and I feel so lonesome that I do not know what to do or whither to turn."

"I suppose, then, I ought to have decreed *you* into exile the other morning."

"Would you, then, have so decided had you accepted our proposition? Would you have sent *me* away?"

"I did not say that. No, no; I was not prepared for that ordeal; but I am sorry Laura has left without saying good-bye to me."

"You love Laura better than you do me, then, do you?"

"No, I do not."

Frances blushed and looked steadily into my eyes for a moment, and then said, in measured words:

"Samuel, Laura Ferris is a precious good girl, and you could never find a worthier object of your love than she is."

"Frances," I said, imitating her sober, measured enunciation, "that is very true, but you, too, are a precious good girl, and no man, be he ever so good, will ever find a worthier object of his love than you."

"You are bound to turn everything serious into ridicule, Sam," she said, "and I confess I don't know how to take you. You are an enigma." And she left the room, and I was once more alone with my thoughts.

"A noble young woman is Frances Wilkins; and what a queenly wife she would be for a good and true man!" This was the whispered thought of my soul when, shortly afterward, I took my hat and left the house for a lonely stroll in the park. "I think much of her, but do I *love* her, and does she love me?" I asked myself, as I walked along, moodily. "And yet Laura, also, is a very lovely girl, and more vivacious, and apparently has more *heart* than Frances."

I must confess the truth, that unconsciously I found myself actually debating, in my own thoughts, the comparitive merits of my two sisterly friends, and the more I debated, the less able I was to form a definite opinion as to which of them I loved best, or, rather, which of them, if either, I would choose for a wife. I gradually became involved in an inextricable quandary, which, from that indecisive evening, grew more and more troublesome to me. I felt that I loved them both, but could not decide which of them I loved the most.

A CLIENT.

CHAPTER IV.

THINGS come out very queerly sometimes. One morning, several days after the events recorded in the foregoing chapter an elderly gentleman came into my office.

" Is Mr. Traverse, the lawyer, in ?"

" I am that man," I modestly responded.

I was entirely alone, and had just finished writing out my points in the case of the Landlord *vs.* Tenant, in which I had been retained by the poor fellow who was in the clutches of an unconscionable old shark, who was oppressing him beyond reason or justice. Let me say here, before I forget it, that, by my assistance, the poor tenant won his case the next day.

"You're the man, eh?" said the old gentleman. "Younger man than I thought to find, and yet I am told you will give me honest and safe advice."

"I never give any but honest professional advice," I replied; "but as to its safety, that, perhaps, is another matter. We have to take the chances on that sometimes."

"Ah! I see; I see," said he, taking a very sharp look at me from under his old-fashioned spectacles.

"Well," he continued, presently, "I have an honest case, and all I ask is honest counsel. You are well up in the laws of the state, I suppose, and if you are, that's all I ask. The question is a simple one of equity and justice; a question of trespass. I own a large farm down in Trowbridge township, county of Winston, and my cattle broke through the fence into my neighbor's wheat-field, in the night-time. I am willing to pay him for actual damage done, but he is not satisfied with reason, and demands four

times the amount that's just. This is the case.
Will you undertake to advise me, and, in the
event of a suit at law, will you conduct the case
for me in court? And do you think you can
prevent his recovering from me more than just
damages ?"

"I can promise you, sir, that I will do my very
best. Your aggrieved neighbor cannot, by any
possibility, recover from you more than just
damages, based upon a careful and reasonable
estimate of the actual value of the property
injured or destroyed."

"That's how it strikes me," rejoined the old
gentleman; "all I want is justice and reason,
and you talk just as I think about it. Now, I
want you to come to my farm, down in Trowbridge, and look the ground over, see the cattle,
the fence, and the wheat-field, and then look up
the law, and advise me, honest and fair, what I
ought to do."

"I will do that, certainly, if you desire it, and
yet I am entirely unacquainted with agricultural

matters, the value of fences or wheat-fields, and could, upon your own information, probably give you just as good advice here as if I should visit and inspect the premises."

But, as many a lawyer will attest, there is no use trying to convince a man of hard-headed "justice," such as my present visitor was, that anything could be done, even in a law-suit, without first examining the geography, the topography, and the tangible and visible details of the premises of the whole matter and circumstances; and so, agreeably to his request, I consented that on a certain day I would visit his farm, over an hundred miles distant, and scrutinize the physical situation of the origin of the neighborly controversy.

Now, this may seem like traversing out of the way when one is telling a love story. A case of trespass, involving principles of law and equity, would seem to be quite a different matter from that involved in the question that the motherly Mrs. Wilkins and her two dear girls wished me to decide. But wait and see. As I said, things come about very queerly sometimes.

A PROFESSIONAL TRIP.

CHAPTER V.

IT was a bright summer day when I took the train and ran down to the township of Trowbridge, county of Winston. At the station-house I was met by the old farmer, (whose name, I must not forget to tell you, was Jones,) and I found that all his neighbors and the folks round about called him " Deacon," and that he was a great man in his district. Deacon Jones drove me, in a double carriage, straight to his house, a mile distant, and, in a very business-like way, at once proceeded to the veritable fence through which his cattle had broken into that veritable wheat-field, for the injury to the growing grain in which his aggrieved neighbor

4

demanded unreasonable damages. It is not necessary to our purpose to go into details as to our examination of the premises, our estimates of the actual injury done, or the probable market value of the wheat destroyed. It was very apparent to me that Deacon Jones was a fair, reasonable man, who honestly desired to settle the controversy with his neighbor upon a just and honorable basis.

"Should Mr. Bingle," (that was the name of the Deacon's aggrieved neighbor,) "should Mr. Bingle attempt, by suit at law, to recover more than the sum of damages you have offered him," I said, "I will guaranty his failure of success. No jury of farmers would award him as much as you offer him; of that I am satisfied."

"That's just what I told him yesterday," remarked the Deacon, "and yet he threatens to sue."

And the old gentleman, who informed me that never in all his long life had he been a party to a lawsuit, and never wished to be, sighed deeply, looked sad, and invited me to his house. On our way thither he took occasion to tell me how much this little neighborly quarrel had troubled him, and how he wished Mr. Bingle could be persuaded to see that "right is right, and justice is justice," and settle the matter on "the square," without any further difficulty. I proposed that he send for Mr. Bingle, and we would talk it over quietly with him, then and there.

"No," he replied, "Bingle is a singular sort of a fellow, and wouldn't come over if I should send for him. The only way is for us to go over to his house and 'beard the lion in his den!'"

"Well, let us do that, then," I proposed, and it was so agreed; and in the latter part of the day the Deacon and I walked across the fields of the adjoining farms to Mr. Bingle's.

Mr. Bingle, sure enough, was a singular sort of man; crabbed, unsociable, repellent. He did not propose to compromise; didn't believe in compromises, any way — and I was a little amused in hearing him repeat, almost word for word, the sentiment of my client, that "right is right, and justice is justice."

And here is a question that, in personal controversies, is often very difficult to answer: What is right — what is justice? I left the two disputants to discuss the question in their neighborly, but ill-natured way, and sat quietly in a corner of the big room.

"Heaven help us," I said to myself, as I sat alone, "what *is* right and just? Here are two men of more than ordinary sense trying to persuade each other — one that he has been damaged overmuch, the other that his neighbor's claim is unreasonable — and I the arbitrator. Heaven help me and justice, for I see that I have now been placed in the breach to decide between these two quarreling neighbors." And I tried to comprehend the entire situation, and endeavored, after having heard both sides, to conclude in my own mind how to advise my client, the good Deacon, honestly, as to what was best, safest and right. For an hour I kept my silent corner, and finally reached a conclusion, based not only upon reason, but upon law. I knew, because I saw and understood, that Deacon Jones was not only disposed to do right and to satisfy his unreasonable neighbor, but that he would even, if need be, go far beyond reason and justice in order to prevent a public suit at law.

" Now, Mr. Bingle," I said, coming back from my silent corner, after having heard the statements and asseverations of both sides of the case, and the argumentations of each to persuade the other that he was right and the other wrong, "Mr. Bingle, while I have been regularly employed by Mr. Jones to represent his interest in this controversy, yet I candidly assure you that, after talking very freely with him before, and listening to your discussion now, I am sure—quite and entirely positive—that he wishes to do *right*. And what more can you or he, or anybody, desire in such a case? Mr. Jones tells me that he is heartily sorry that his cattle broke over his fence, entering and destroying your wheat-field. I believe his expression of regret is sincere. And after doing his very best to compute the actual damage done, he proposes to settle with you honorably. His basis of settlement, I think, is that of a just man; no court in the world would award to you honester or juster terms than he proposes. Think of his proposition seriously, and accept it. It would be honest—it would be neighborly—it would be the right thing to do as between man and man."

Thus relieving myself—and I spoke very frankly and earnestly—I "fell back in good order," as the soldiers used to say in the war, and left the two quarreling farmers to reach a conclusion. They talked the matter over again; they argued and re-argued, agreed and disagreed, but failed to come to an understanding. Finally, from my corner, to which I had again retreated, and where I was trying to read a newspaper, I heard this remark, delivered very emphatically by Mr. Bingle: " Deacon, my niece, Loll, (you know her,) is a mighty smart young woman — I'll agree to leave the whole matter to her, and what she says I'll agree to, and she knows nothing at all about it now, I warrant you."

"Loll! Loll!! What does she know about matters of this kind?" I heard the Deacon ask, and then advanced to the scene of the dual strife and suggested to my client thus: "Mr. Jones, the intuitions of woman are always on the side of justice and right — accept his proposition."

"I'll do it," instantly exclaimed Deacon Jones; "I'll do it, and yet I don't know how capable she is of deciding anything. I want peace and good neighborhood, and will do almost anything to settle this trouble to mutual satisfaction."

Mr. Bingle at once went out of the room, saying, "I'll bring Loll; she's quick to see a thing; her decision will be right, and right is all I want."

It was a spectacle worth the seeing—it was indeed—to see those two old farmers endeavoring to settle their petty differences in their peculiar way; and, for a lawyer, accustomed to the ways and means of legal controversy, it was not only amusing, but afforded an opportunity for a profitable lesson. It was — so I then thought—an excellent exhibition of human nature in its unsophisticated state. Both gentlemen were intelligent, as the world goes, and their opinions would, no doubt, have been accepted as equal to law by their rustic friends and neighbors, for many miles around, on ordinary matters of question; but *this* was not an ordinary matter — it was *extraordinary* — and so they kept it from their neighbors and friends, and none knew of their controversy but their two immediate families and myself; and I must acknowledge that, youthful barrister and inexperienced in family or neighborhood squabbles as I then was, I would have given almost anything in the world that was at my command, if I could have taken myself entirely out of the quarrel. But it was too late. Deacon Jones had deliberately drawn me into it as his advisor and counsel, and, as a young lawyer, with nothing behind him but great hopes, and with great ambition before him, I was professionally bound, as the saying is in the American idiom, to "see the thing through," and to bring my client out of the difficulty with honor and legal justice.

I sat for five minutes in the solemn and silent presence of the grave old Deacon, when Mr. Bingle re-entered the drawing-room with his niece Loll, when I again retreated to my corner in the back part of the great room.

"Loll?" I instinctively exclaimed to myself — "Loll? Why, it's Laura Ferris — it's the niece of Mrs. Wilkins — it's one of my dear sisters at my home in Westerly!"

"My niece, Loll," said Mr. Bingle to Deacon Jones. "This, Loll, is the gentleman whose farm is next adjoining ours, with whom we have a dispute about damages."

"Mr. Jones," said Loll, "I have often seen

and heard of you, and I know your daughter, Mary, very well; we are excellent friends, and my uncle and you must have no unpleasant disagreements between you. Uncle tells me that you two have a trouble, and he wants me to decide between you. It's very funny to me; the very idea. I promise you that when I shall give my decision, I will decide in your favor, Mr. Jones, on Mary's account, and I know that will be the end of it, for you think very much of your Mary, and uncle, here, thinks very much of me, and we two families cannot afford to be put out with each other; it would be dreadful, it would indeed."

"But," said ⁕Deacon Jones, "there is a question of right and justice involved in the matter, and it must be decided righteously, so that both shall be satisfied."

"That is just what I told Loll," said Mr. Bingle, "when I requested her to come in, hear the matter, and decide between us. Loll is a bright, good, honest girl, and her judgment, whatever it be, will be right, I know."

Just then, seeing a favorable opportunity, I advanced toward them from out of my corner, and remarked : "Mr. Jones, it is all right—trust to Loll's judgment—I'll be security for her any day."

"Why, Sam!—Sam Traverse! dear brother Sam! How came you here?" exclaimed Laura Ferris—for it was indeed the sprightly Laura, with her auburn curls and blue eyes — who, to my sadness, had left our home at Westerly only a week or two ago, without even bidding me good-bye, to spend some weeks with her grandmother, here, at her uncle's. The grandmother, —Mrs. Summerfield—was the mother of Mr. Bingle's wife, now dead.

Do you see, now, reader, how things happen queerly sometimes? I do not know why it happened thus. But other queer incidents are still to be told.

MOONLIGHT MEDITATIONS.

CHAPTER VI.

MOONLIGHT MEDITATIONS.

IT was a delightful moonlight evening in the country. In the country! There is to my mind something so captivating, so very charming about the country, in contradistinction from the town or city—something so much like the difference between Paradise and Pandemonium—that I wonder—or, at least, I did wonder at this time—how people could live anywhere but in the country, especially in the summer time, and while the moon is shining in the quiet evenings.

I spent that evening in a moonlight walk with Laura along the shaded highway. I will never forget the pleasures of that hour as long as I live. Laura was the very paragon of loveliness;

amiable, affectionate, confiding. How could any man, born of woman, and sent forth into the world with the blessings of a revered woman upon his head, take a walk, spend an evening, and interchange thought and sentiment with such as she without loving her? Men are human, the greatest and the least of them, and so are women. Bring them together alone— especially on a moonlight evening in the country —and their humanity is irresistible. On that evening Laura and I parted at the door of her uncle Bingle's mansion as lovingly as the most devoted of human creatures. I knew she loved me, because she declared it in enthusiastic words, and I felt that I loved her. Heaven help us at such a time, for we, poor weaklings, cannot help ourselves. I told Laura that she was the idol of my soul. And it was so. At least I thought so then.

A WOMAN'S JUDGMENT.

CHAPTER VII.

A WOMAN'S JUDGMENT.

I WAS an invited guest the next day at the mansion of Mr. Bingle.

"Well, Loll," said Mr. Bingle, "have you decided in your mind the matter between the Deacon and I? It is time—what's your judg—ment? Is he or I right? Come, let me know, for I have agreed to take you and 'Lawyer Sam,' as you call him, over there to-night to spend the evening and come to a final settlement, one way or 'tother."

"Uncle," she replied, "I honestly confess to you that since Sam has arrived here, I have not been able to think a serious thought. I know him so well that, without thinking anything at all about it, I know that whatever he advises is right.   Do as he says—that's my decision."

"But, Loll," the brusque old gentleman retorted, "this Lawyer Sam is here as the adviser of Deacon Jones, and is in his interest.   That won't do.   The Deacon is unreasonable, and Sam supports him, and all I want is right and justice.   Now, Loll, you know all about it—we have told you—and I look to you to decide wisely and justly, from your own knowledge of the matter."

"Uncle," she said, "if you knew Sam as well as I do, you would tell him to settle the matter as he thinks best, and there let it rest.   He will do justly—I know he will.   I would trust to his judgment rather than my own, and so may you. And this, dear uncle, is my decision—that whatever Sam Traverse shall declare right and just, is so, and must be so—he is an honest man if ever there has been one in the world."

The old gentleman turned away frowningly. He did not like this unexpected climax, and

evidently felt that the close friendship between
his niece and Deacon Jones' lawyer was a conspiracy on the part of the Deacon. And Laura,
with the quick, instinctive perception of a woman,
at once discovered this suspicion in his mind,
and, leaving me abruptly alone, she followed him
into his room. Presently returning, she said :
" That matter is settled, at all events ; my uncle
must not think me a party against him—and
now, when we go over to Deacon Jones' this
evening, you must let me announce the verdict
in this affair, which they have left to me, for
neither my uncle nor the Deacon must think
that you have influenced me. You have said
nothing to me about it, but I understand it all.
Leave it to me, and I will see that justice is
done."

I, knowing her innate honesty and shrewdness,
acquiesced without a dissenting word.

In the evening uncle Bingle, Laura and I
walked leisurely across the fields to the mansion
of Deacon Jones. It was a charming evening,

and even the crabbed uncle, walking at the side
of his sprightly niece, became somewhat senti-
mental, and in a sad, half-youthful sort of mood,
referred to the delightful walks and heavenly
communions that he and that "precious wife"
of his, who had "gone to heaven," used to have
on just such evenings and nights as this. And I
looked in the old gentleman's face as we strolled
along, and saw something glistening on his cheek
that looked very like a tear, and I took him by
the arm and said, softly, "God help us all, Mr.
Bingle: we all are weak and helpless creatures;
uncertainty, death, and heart-troubles are the
destiny of every one of us. I honor the tear
that a sacred memory calls up ; it tells of a good
heart. God bless you, Mr. Bingle!"

The old gentleman drew his handkerchief
across his face, and, after walking silently for a
few minutes, exclaimed:

"Why, why, Loll! Loll! does this lawyer Sam
love you, and do you love him? Now come, tell
me." His voice was husky and trembeld like

that of a weeping woman. His eyes were full
of tears, and, stopping, he looked into Laura's
face and then into mine, with a peculiar eager-
ness.

"We love each other, uncle," Laura said, "as
brother and sister—that is all—that is all."

"Lawyer Sam," he said, resuming our walk,
"is that all? Tell me truly, for I see you are a
good fellow, and Loll, here, is a good girl—a
very, very good girl. Her mother, who was my
wife's sister, was just like her."

"She has told you all there is between us," I
replied.

He kissed his niece, and then pressed my
hand. Crabbed old fellow as he was, we had
found the human part of him. But he thought
Laura and I were more and nearer to each other
than we really were. I do not know what
Laura thought, but I remember very well what I
thought.

Presently we reached Deacon Jones' gate, and
found that grave-faced gentleman awaiting us.

He received us cordially, and after seating us in his parlor, called in his wife and daughter and introduced us to them.   Mrs. Jones was a motherly-appearing dame, more youthful in looks than in years, with a few straggling gray hairs in a profusion of dark curls which graced both sides of a sunny face.   Her daughter, Mary— sweet old name!—was a charming young lady of about twenty—a perfect beauty—with a face all sunshine and intelligence;   manners as polished and language as refined as those of the most cultivated of the city belles;   her dark hair tastefully arranged over a broad brow that was as white as marble, and large dark-brown eyes beaming dreamily from a well-rounded physiognomy.

I confess to a peculiar admiration for beautiful women—an admiration that amounts almost to an infatuation—an admiration that always has been with me a pleasurable enthusiasm, if not a positive weakness.   And it is not a confession to be ashamed of.   Is there anything in animated nature that is more beautiful than a really beautiful woman—a woman well-formed physically, with an angelic face, a good heart and mind, and a pure soul—a woman combining facial charms with refined sensibilities, modesty, neatness, gentleness? I don't mean your gaudy creations of art and affectation—not those whose beauty consists only of their apparel and the tricks and appliances of fashion. The beauty of these is not the beauty of women, but the ingenuity of art—it is all on the surface, and generally all is emptiness within. Neither do I mean those whose faces are fair, whose hair is profuse and well ordered, whose eyes are bright, or whose manners are winning; these are essential elements, perhaps, but something more is needed to complete my ideal of a beautiful woman—such as culture, good sense, and moral loveliness. A really beautiful woman must be a good woman, a pure, chaste, modest woman, as well as handsome physically—she must be truly womanly and truly lovely. And when I meet

such an one, I do not try to resist her charms—
I cannot—they are irresistible—and I yield
myself her captive at once and unconditionally.
Beautiful women, such as I mean, were Laura,
Frances and my newly-discovered divinity, Mary
Jones.

"Well, neighbor Jones," slowly and solemnly
opened Mr. Bingle, after a few minutes of preliminary conversation around the little circle,
"we have come over to settle our little dispute,
as appointed, and as 'business before pleasure'
is a good rule, I propose that we come to that at
once, and end all further misunderstanding."

"The sooner the better, as far as I am concerned, Mr. Bingle," said Deacon Jones, rising
nervously from his chair; "is your niece ready
to make the decision? We have left it all to
her, I believe."

"Yes," said Laura, "my verdict is prepared,
and it is this: That you two good old neighbors
shall make up and be friends. You, Mr. Jones,
shall pay my uncle nothing at all, and you, my

dear uncle, shall say to Mr. Jones something like
this : ' My good Deacon, your cattle broke into
my wheat-field and damaged my grain—it was
very annoying, and I became much incensed;
but you were not to blame for it. Some time
my cattle may break into one of your fields in
the same way. These things do happen sometimes, especially between farmers who are neighbors. So, if at any time my cattle should annoy
or do damage to you, I would expect that you
would be as considerate toward me as I am now
toward you. As neighbors, let us be friends,
and treat each other as Christian neighbors and
friends should.' "

Laura spoke these words as deliberately as a
preacher would his sermon, and with all the
quiet gesture, emphasis and grace that an actress
would deliver a studied speech on the stage.
Then bowing to her uncle and Deacon Jones,
she concluded : " This is my verdict : it may not
be business-like, as you would say, but I feel and
know it is neighbor-like and Christian-like."

I could not help it, but when she concluded I
instinctively clapped my hands applaudingly
and exclaimed: "Bravo, Laura! bravo!" And
Miss Mary Jones, her eyes brimfull of smiles,
joined me, clapping her hands also, and exclaimed, "Laura, you would make a first-rate
Judge!" And then Deacon Jones spoke up:
"I am afraid this verdict is a little one-sided,
my good lady—so much so, indeed, that I hardly
know what to make of it, or how to take it.
Mr. Bingle, I suspect you have caused your niece
to play a little joke here at my expense, or,
rather, at your expense. How is it?"

All eyes were now turned toward Mr. Bingle.
I could see the same peculiarly sad expression
on his face that I noted when, speaking of his
dead wife while we were walking through the
fields that evening, his eyes filled with tears and
his voice trembled like a woman's. He sat
silent and unmoved for a moment—first looked
intently at Laura, then at me, then at the
Deacon. "It is no joke of mine," he remarked,

slowly and nervously, at last: "I knew not what her decision would be until she declared it. But it is all right—the dear girl is right—so like her aunt, my sainted wife—so like her· so like the spirit of a true Christian. I thank you, Laura, and, Mr. Jones, I beg your forgiveness for not having until this moment seen my duty as a neighbor more clearly. Loll is right; it is just as her aunt would have advised if she were living. It is all right."

And the old gentleman, wiping a tear from his cheek, arose, grasped his neighbor by the hand, and they were friends again, and better friends than they had ever been before, and truer and better neighbors from that time forward.

"I sent for you, Mr. Traverse, to come and help me settle this quarrel, as a lawyer," remarked Deacon Jones, taking my hand, "and now tell me, did Laura act under your advice, or was this her own device?"

"I assure you, and also Mr. Bingle," I replied, "that Laura and I have not exchanged a single word in reference to the dispute. She neither asked me anything concerning it, nor did I presume to mention it to her, or to make even a suggestion. I approve the judgment entirely, but most emphatically deny having influenced the mind of the judge."

"A remarkable young woman!" said Deacon Jones.

"Indeed she *is* a remarkable young woman," joined Mr. Bingle—"so like her aunt who is dead—so very, very like."

"Now let us dismiss this whole matter from our conversation and minds," said Laura; "it is settled; all are satisfied, and I am the most gratified of all concerned, for I know I have decided justly, and am rejoiced to see that you all think so. Here, Mr. Traverse, I want you to know my friend Mary well—for she and I are good friends, and have been ever since we were little children."

And we three young folks of the party retired into an adjoining room, leaving the Deacon and his wife and Mr. Bingle to themselves in the parlor, as sociable and happy as old neighbors should be, and the happier for the removal of the subject of the late dispute.

It was a very pleasant evening. I enjoyed the society of Mary Jones and Laura greatly; we had a lively conversation at first, then social games, and then a frolic by moonlight on the lawn and in the garden. I must candidly acknowledge that there was something about Mary Jones that irresistibly captivated me. Laura was sprightly, pretty and loving, but Mary was all these and something more—and that something—call it intellectuality, call it culture, or call it magnetism—drew me to her as I thought I had never been drawn to a woman before. And, somehow, before the evening was over, I felt that I *loved* Mary Jones, and I saw and felt that the sentiment found a response in her own soul. Laura Ferris did not know it—dear creature—nobody else under the sky knew it or suspected it; but it was so, and when taking my

departure that night from the house of my
client, Deacon Jones—for Laura and her uncle
insisted that I must be their guest for another
day—there was a mutual pressure of hands
when Mary and I said good night, and a very
cordial expression of a hope that we would soon
meet again.

"It is all right," said Mr. Bingle, as we were
returning across the fields, "it is all right, Loll,
and I am glad you decided just as you did. I
am a better man for it, and the Deacon and I
will be better friends and neighbors for it. It is
all right—so like your aunt, my dear dead wife—
so like her—so very like her. Lawyer Sam,"
that is what he persisted in calling me, "you
will never find a better girl than Loll. She tells
me that you and she are as brother and sister.
That cannot be so long, and I half suspect it is
more than that now. Come, now, tell me, isn't
there something more serious between you?"

"We have boarded together so long with her
aunt in town," I replied, "that we have indeed

become like brother and sister. I did not dream
of meeting her out here when I came to Trowbridge, at Deacon Jones' request, yet meeting
her has made my visit exceedingly pleasant.
We are very good friends, Mr. Bingle—Laura
and I—but nothing more, I think—eh, Laura?"

"That is all, uncle—only good friends, like
brother and sister—but "—

"But?" repeated Mr. Bingle, "but what?"

"Oh, nothing, uncle—nothing; I did not know
what I was going to say." And I could see, by
the soft light of the moon, that a blush suffused
those fresh round cheeks—and I was troubled
again, for I knew what she was thinking about—
I recollected what she and I had talked about
so affectionately during our romantic moonlight
walk on the previous evening. It was love.

Again I was confronted by the question,
Which do I love best? This time it was not
Laura Ferris or Frances Wilkins—it was Mary
Jones or Laura Ferris. Laura was beautiful,
affectionate, good, sensible—and I was sure I

6

did love her last evening; but why did she give Mary Jones and me an opportunity to know each other so well this evening? I was beginning to distrust myself. Was I fickle and heartless? Was I the ready victim of every pretty face and loving smile? Did I really know what love was? Was I a simpleton and a fool in these matters? I could not answer these questions, and they continued to keep me awake that night until toward the morning, when I fell asleep and dreamed a beautiful dream—not about Laura Ferris; not about Mary Jones; but about Mrs. Wilkins and her majestic, dark-eyed daughter, Frances.

The next day, reluctantly bidding Laura and her uncle good-bye, I returned to Westerly and my office—to Mrs. Wilkins and Frances.

AN OLD CHUM'S ADVICE.

CHAPTER VIII.

AN OLD CHUM'S ADVICE.

ONE of the first persons to enter my office, after my return from Trowbridge, was my old college chum and intimate friend, Joe Startling. Joe was a young man — about my own age, a noble fellow, and unmarried. He was now a merchant, doing business in Westerly.

"Joe," said I, after commonplace conversation, "why don't you marry?"

"Queer question for you to ask me," he replied, "Sam, why don't *you* marry?"

"Can't afford it, but you can — that's the difference."

"I might afford it," he said, "but I have yet to find the woman. But, Sam, why did you ask me this question?"

"For the purpose of asking you another. If there were two or three ladies, all young, beautiful and lovely, from whom you could choose a wife —you esteeming them equally, and knowing that they either do or could love you — how would you decide, if you felt it a duty to decide between them?"

"Were I placed in that situation, I would decide very quickly. I would choose the best and prettiest of them, everything else being equal — that is, if I loved her and was sure she loved me."

"But supposing they were equally good and equally pretty, and that you esteemed them equally, and were aware that each of them loved you, or would if you desired it."

"That," replied Joe, smiling, "is not a possible combination of conditions."

And then I unbosomed myself to Joe, whom I had always found a safe depository of my secrets, and a good adviser withal. I told him all about Frances Wilkins and Laura Ferris and my new-found friend Mary Jones.

" I know all three of them," said Joe, when I had told him all, " and most excellent girls they are — none better, none prettier, none lovelier; but were I in your place, Sam, I would take Laura Ferris. That speech of hers, when deciding the question between the two farmers, if she acquitted herself as you have just stated, shows that she would make an excellent wife for an honest lawyer — she would be a helpmeet — and she is a very pretty, sweet girl."

Somehow I felt that Joe spoke wisely, and yet, after he had gone, I gradually fell into as grave a quandary as ever. I thought of the fine form and winning face I saw and admired at Deacon Jones' — of those smiling eyes that spake back to mine and seemed to fascinate my very soul. And then I thought of the majestic and womanly Frances, whom I had known so long and so well, and whose qualities of mind and temper I could not but acknowledge and admire. The more I thought of the three divinities, the more I was puzzled to decide which I should set up as my particular idol.

A RIVAL.

CHAPTER IX.

IN the evening, on entering Mrs. Wilkins' drawing room, I met there a stranger — a tall, black-haired, black-bearded, fine appearing man — somewhat older than I, apparently — and whom Mrs. Wilkins introduced to me as Mr. Gentry, a friend, who had come from an Eastern city to spend a day or two with them. He and I soon became sociable. I liked him. He was a man of intelligence, affable and gentlemanly. We talked about everything — the topics of current news — the weather, literature — the latest developments in science — business — and got along together very finely, agreeing in sentiment, generally, and differing only in the details of the

topics of our conversation and discussion. Indeed I found him a very pleasant gentleman,
and he politely informed me that, having some
time ago gone out of trade, he was now a cap-
italist—a loaner of money, his income being a
handsome per cent. on a very snug amount.

I liked Mr. Gentry very well, and was getting
to like him better every moment, when our conversation was interrupted by the entrance of
Frances.

"I'm glad to see such good friends of mine
taking to each other so readily," she said. "And
now, without wishing to be rude, please tell me
what you are talking about so earnestly."

"Everything — nothing — anything," replied
Mr. Gentry, rising and taking her hand; "but
now what would *you* talk about?"

"Everything — nothing — anything," she retorted, laughing; "but Mr. Traverse should tell
us where he has been these few days past, what
he has seen, and all about it."

"It would be too long a story," I said; "nothing remarkable — a professional mission, but one of its most remarkable incidents was the meeting of Laura at her uncle's."

Instantly, after saying this, I discovered that her face flushed, and immediately I could see a change in her entire manner toward me. Instead of seeking my side, as had been her wont, she moved away from me, and I could see a troubled expression in her eye. It did not take long for me to discover what the matter was. The jealous young woman actually got the notion into her head that I had gone off to visit her cousin Laura, and that this was the occasion of my absence from town. Aware, as I soon became, that this gentleman, Mr. Gentry, had come as an admirer of Frances — a wooer — I readily perceived that I was the third person who could very conveniently be spared from the company, in order to complete the pleasure of the other two. At the earliest opportunity I excused myself, and left the room.

The rest of that evening I occupied in arguing

two questions, the first of which was whether, under the circumstances, it was my duty to explain to Frances Wilkins my visit to the town of Trowbridge, and my accidental and unexpected meeting there with her cousin Laura; the other was, whether this apparently clever gentleman, Mr. Gentry, would not, in any event, prove a successful rival for the hand of Frances, even if I should wish to aspire to it.   I went to bed that night, feeling wretched — and falling asleep after an hour or two of vexatious thought, I dreamed — I always have been a great dreamer — that Frances Wilkins had grown cold toward me — no longer called me " brother Sam "— and was promenading affectionately with that handsome, black-bearded Mr. Gentry, right in front of my own office, apparently with the express object of exciting my ire and jealousy. And then, in my dream, I forgot this trouble by meeting Laura, and walking with her across the green fields and in the shade of the silent groves of the Trowbridge farm, by the romantic moonlight — lovingly pledging her my whole heart, and she reciprocating my every word of love and promise. And then, somehow, the dream closed amid the flower-beds and shrubbery of Deacon Jones' dooryard, with Mary Jones gently and sweetly beckoning me to her side, her eyes shining like big diamonds, and her cheeks as rosy and velvety as the leaves of the blooming dahlias that shed their silent beauty on the scene around. She beckoned to me very, very earnestly, I dreamed, to come to her, but Laura's hand, linked firmly in my arm, kept me back, and in the struggle of an undecided and divided will and purpose, I awakened — and discovering that it was all a dream, I, somehow, was impelled to thank my stars that it was so. And yet, thinking further, I said to myself: "A dream no doubt it is, but very like a reality. Which of those three women *do* I love the most?"

FRIENDSHIP, LOVE AND JEALOUSY.

CHAPTER X.

"SAM," said my old friend and chum, Joe Startling, meeting me on the street several days after the events already narrated, "how about that trio of lovely young damsels you told me about the other day? Have you made a choice between them yet?"

"No, no : and I am troubled almost to death about them. The struggle is as terrible as ever, and I am as undecided as ever. I have just had a pleasant talk with Mrs. Wilkins, my motherly landlady, and she thinks me a fool."

"I don't know but she is right, Sam," he said, laughing; "a man who doesn't know his own mind, and can't decide what his own tastes and preferences are, is not far from being a fool."

"But, Joe," I said, warming up at this impeachment of my manhood, "you acknowledged to me the other day that if it was your case you wouldn't know how to decide. True, you advised Laura as the best woman for an honest lawyer's wife, but how do you know that either of the other two wouldn't be just as good a wife for an honest lawyer? Both are fine ladies, possessed of every quality that a good man would desire in a good woman."

"Nonsense, man!" he exclaimed, seriously, "if you have a mind of your own—if you have power of judgment—you can, if you really know what love is, decide this matter, and the sooner you do it the better. I know you well enough to know that if you permit a matter of this kind to trouble you, it will monopolize your best thoughts, and be a serious obstacle in the way of your professional success, which, at your time of life, is everything. Decide at once, and let that be the end—that is, if you are sure the one of your choice loves you, and that you love her.

There, now, bachelor as I am, you have my views plainly, and honestly, too, I assure you."

I saw that Joe was sincere. He meant every word he said. Just then a thought struck me.

"Joe," I said, "you know these three young ladies, of whom I have told you. Now I have a favor to ask of you. Will you accompany me, next Saturday night, to the town of Trowbridge, to spend Sunday there, and spend one evening at Deacon Jones', where we will meet his daughter Mary, and also one evening at his neighbor Bingle's, where we will meet Laura Ferris?"

Joe hesitated a moment, and finally consented. It was agreed that we would, on the next Saturday, go to Trowbridge, returning the next Monday morning.

No sooner had Joe left my office than a post-boy entered the door and handed me a letter. Opening it, I found, to my gratification, that it was from Mary Jones. It was written in an elegant hand, and read as follows :

"TROWBRIDGE, August 15, 18—.
"Mr. Samuel Traverse:

"DEAR SIR—Acting in the capacity of my father's Secretary, I enclose herewith, at his request, a check, which he desires you to accept for the service you have rendered him professionally. He trusts it will be satisfactory.

"In my own behalf, as well as at my father's request, I very cordially invite you to call, at any time, at our rural home, and become the guest of a family that sincerely esteems you.

"Very respectfully, sir,

"MARY JONES."

It was a neat specimen of feminine chirography, judiciously worded, and I fancied that I could see beneath every word the smiling eyes and the beautiful face of its writer.

"If Joe could see that tastefully-framed little missive," I thought, "he might conclude that Laura Ferris is, after all, not the only young lady who would make an excellent wife for an honest lawyer. I warrant that this farmer's daughter would make any good and true man a good and true wife."

Leaving my office early in the evening, I went to my home at Mrs. Wilkins', and there, sitting alone in the drawing-room, grave and dignified almost to chilliness, I found Frances. Taking her hand, I said, " Frances, what is the matter? Why do you treat me so coldly?"

" I am not accountable for my feelings, Sam," she replied; " I cannot help feeling hurt that, without saying one word to me about it, you should have followed cousin Laura to her uncle's—and that, too, so soon after her departure. Why did you not tell me frankly that you loved her?"

I endeavored, with great gravity, to explain the facts of my going to Trowbridge, and assured her that meeting Laura there was the merest accident; but I could see by her looks and her manner that she doubted my story, which piqued me greatly, and the fact that, without saying much more, she covered her face with her hands and left the room sobbing, did not add to my comfort the least. Presently I heard her mother in the adjoining room, and, calling to her, tried to explain the whole matter to her, expressing regret at Frances' suspicions and reproaches. She seemed to sympathize with me, remarking, "Don't let it trouble you, my son—it's one of those little lovers' quarrels which never last long." But, somehow, I thought I could discover even in the old lady's looks, as we were speaking, that which told me she, too, doubted me, and that she, too, felt annoyed with me.

We three sat down to tea that evening as unsocially almost as if we had been strangers. Few words were spoken, and those merely conventional. There were no demonstrations, looks or words indicating unfriendliness, but there was wanting that freedom and cordiality which had always hitherto characterized our intercourse, both at the table and in the drawing-room. The only speech made by Frances, during the repast, was this: "Mr. Gentry is a very fine gentleman, don't you think so, Sam?"

I replied that, from the slight opportunity I had of making his acquaintance, my impression was very favorable.

" I am glad to hear you say so, my son," spoke up Mrs. Wilkins, " for he is a good friend of ours, and is very fond of Frances."

Never before that moment had I experienced the emotion of jealousy. That last remark of the mother set my blood on fire, and much as I would dislike, even at this day, to do injustice to these good friends of mine, whom I had so long regarded as mother and sister, I could not help but think, as I was pondering over the matter in my own room subsequently, that these remarks about Mr. Gentry were made with the deliberate intention of exciting my jealousy. Those who understand the nature, the arts and the ingenuity of woman better than I did then, will pass their own judgment upon this point.

Suffice it to say that in our subsequent conversations neither the misunderstanding between Frances and myself, nor the name of Mr.

Gentry, was even as much as referred to again.
At the same time it was very evident to me that
Frances was jealous of her cousin Laura, and
that I was jealous of the black-bearded man
who was, as I foolishly felt, encroaching upon
my domain.

On the night after the unsatisfactory evening
at tea, I retired half-provoked, and yet feeling
that Frances Wilkins was too rare a prize to be
given up. I sank to sleep, and, as usual, got to
dreaming, and this time my dream was of
Frances and that black-bearded man. I
thought that he came to steal her away from me,
and that, catching him in the act, I seized and
throttled him unmercifully, and that then
Frances turned fiercely upon me, calling me a
"cowardly wretch." And that was all of that
dream I now remember, or care to recall—it
made me miserable for days afterward. Not
that I believed in dreams— for I did not, and do
not now—deeming them as nothing more or less
than the wild pranks of the imagination when

the reason, its keeper, is dormant; but the terrible rebuke conveyed by the fierce look and the withering epithet from so unexpected a source sent a terror to my very soul, from which I did not soon wholly recover.

IN THE COUNTRY.

CHAPTER XI.

PROMPTLY at the appointed time on the next Saturday, Joe Startling entered my office, ready for the journey by railway to Trowbridge, which station we reached an hour before sunset. Engaging quarters at a hotel at the little village clustered around the station, after partaking of refreshments, we started for the farm-house of Deacon Jones, which we reached after a leisurely walk of half an hour. We found the good old Deacon at home—also, his wife— likewise his daughter. Our visit was, of course, quite unexpected, but our welcome was none the less cordial. Mary Jones was delightful— buoyant in spirits, brilliant in conversation, and beautiful as an angel. She would have charmed the most stoical man in the world. The evening passed quickly and joyously, and it was along toward the midnight hour when Joe and I bade the family good night and returned to the station and to our rooms in the hotel.

My plan was for both of us to spend this evening together at Deacon Jones', and the next at Mr. Bingle's, with Laura. By special invitation of the Deacon, we agreed to accompany him and his family to the little church on the hill near by on the ensuing Sunday. He would send his carriage for us, he said, and Mary would drive.

A summer Sabbath-day in the country, when the sky is cloudless, a slight breeze stirring, and a smiling and yet solemn peacefulness pervades all nature, can be fully appreciated only by him who seldom enjoys the luxury. The very birds in the trees seem to have prepared themselves to observe the day with more joyous songs than those they warble on ordinary days; the cattle in

the fields move among the pastures more slowly
and solemnly and lie down in the shade of tree
or grove oftener and longer at a time, and seem
to chew ther cud more leisurely and philosophic-
ally than on other days; the sky looks calmer,
and its blue is deeper, and you can apparently
look farther up into the heaven of our imagination; the men, women and children you meet
are dressed for a holiday, and their humanity
beams in their countenances and exposes itself
in their walks and conversation as on no other
day; the people with good hearts and good con-
sciences feel better on that day, in the country,
and are really nearer God and Heaven. Sunday in a large town is no Sabbath at all as compared to that of the country, with its calm, quiet
and quieting influences, its simple-hearted inhabitants, its sumptuousness of nature, its freedom from art, its thousand glories of earth and
sky and air and stream. Happy they who live
in the great, broad, peaceful country, where
there is no crowding, no elbowing one another,

8

no " style," no empty pretentiousness, no dwarf-
ing conventionalities, on Sunday nor any other
day; but where there is freedom in its broadest
and most beautiful significance, and rest in its
holiest and most refreshing sense.

Feelings and sentiments like these filled our
minds and souls, while on that bright and placid
Sabbath morning, Joe Startling and I strolled
for an hour or two through the fields and groves
and by the side of a modest brook in the
vicinity of Trowbridge Station. Neither of us
accustomed to the country, it was a rare luxury.
We had often seen the country before, but it
never seemed so much like a paradise as on that
lovely August morning. The wild flowers never
bloomed so gaily; the grass never was so green
and soft and luxurious; the birds never sang
and whistled and twittered so joyously; the
summer sun never shone so mercifully, and the
atmosphere of the morning never seemed so
pure and exhilarating.

We walked on until we reached a well-

traveled highway, when, seating ourselves on the
stump of a tree by the wayside to rest, we presently saw a carriage approaching, in which, as it
drew nearer, we could see two occupants—man
and woman; and when it had almost reached
us, I heard a voice and a ringing laugh that
were very familiar to my ear—they were the
voice and the laugh of Laura Ferris. She had
evidently recognized us before we had even suspected seeing friends. The occupants of the
carriage were Mr. Bingle and his niece. The
greeting on both sides and all around was cordial—for Joe was well acquainted with these
friends of mine—and after making due explana-
tion of our happening there at this time, (which
was that we came to spend a quiet day in the
country, and were intending to call at Mr.
Bingle's in the evening,) they insisted that we
must get into their carriage and drive home with
them, Laura saying very earnestly that she had
"something very important" to tell me. Explain-
ing that we had an engagement to accompany

Deacon Jones' family to church that morning, we excused ourselves, and, after promising to meet us at the church, they drove on, leaving Joe and I to retrace our steps to the hotel, where we had scarcely arrived when Miss Mary Jones, alone and beautiful as a peri fresh from Paradise, drove up in a carriage, in which we soon were seated. I offered to take the reins, but she, thanking me, declared she was passionately fond of driving horses, and I must confess that she handled the two spirited chargers with greater skill than I could have managed them—in fact she drove them with the confidence and dexterity of an experienced horseman. Soon we reached the gate of the Jones mansion, where the Deacon was waiting for us. Making some excuse for his wife not accompanying us, as she had intended, he joined us in the capacious family carriage, which was of the olden style, and Mary Jones drove us quickly to the little church on the hill, a mile away.

"A neighbor died this past week," remarked

the Deacon, as we were slowly walking toward the church door, "and the services in the church this forenoon will be in respect to his death. The pastor is absent on his summer vacation, and, by special request, I have.consented to take charge of the services."

A death in the country, like a summer's Sabbath-day in the country, is a more solemn event than is a similar occurrence in a large town. In the country the inhabitants are few and scattered, and when one of them dies a vacancy is made that is both seen and felt; whereas, in the town, where many live, many also die, and one death in the community, even if it be that of an important person, is like the falling of one tree in a dense forest. In the town every man is but a small part of a mass, while in the country there is no mass—every one being in a measure isolated and having a specific identity and oneness. When one dies there, it is like the cutting down or falling down of a tree that had long stood in the middle of a field, where all could see it, and where, having fallen, all would remark it.

The faces of all those who were gathered into the small church were sedate, and you could feel that you were in an atmosphere of sighs and heavyness. The people were sad—they were mourners—the grief of their bosoms was reflected in the solemnity of their countenances. It was a congregation of country people—old men and old women—young men and maidens—and here and there a white-headed boy and a silken-haired girl—all dressed plainly but cleanly, and most of them very neatly.

The time for the opening of the services arrived. An elderly gentleman arose from a front seat and read an old-fashioned hymn; the congregation arose as orderly as a company of soldiers would move to the music of a funeral march, and they sang the mournful old hymn as we were wont to hear it long ago in the village church of our early boyhood. With every note you could hear a sigh—with every pause you could imagine the dropping of tears—with every rise and fall of the combined voices your own heart would swell and relax in sympathy with the emotions of the sorrowing friends. The hymn sang, the congregation solemnly sank down into the seats again, and then, after a short pause, Deacon Jones arose and advanced to the front of the pulpit.

"Good neighbors and friends," he said, slowly, and with a trembling voice, "we have assembled in this holy temple at this time to give expression in words to the emotions of our hearts, at the death of our old neighbor, Mr. Fergus, who departed this life on last Wednesday, and whose lifeless form now lies buried in yonder graveyard. You all knew him as we all know each other. A good man—honorable in all the dealings and relations of life—a Christian by profession and in practice—a faithful citizen, a peaceful, kindly neighbor—the deceased commanded and received our respect, our esteem, and our confidence. The sadness of our hearts—our silent tears—our unaffected sorrow witness the greatness of our conscious loss by his death."

Then, wiping the big tears from his cheeks, and pausing for a moment to suppress emotions that could with difficulty be controlled, he resumed :

"And what more can we say—what more need be said—except to apply to ourselves the lesson which the occasion teaches?   He has only taken, in advance of us, the road which we all must take at last—the path that leads down into the grave.   He has gone only a few days, or at best only a very few years, before us.   Let us pray God that we may go as peacefully, hap. pily as he has—that we may be as well prepared as he was to meet our Creator in eternity."

The Deacon spake these few appropriate words very slowly and impressively, and when he sat down almost every head in that congrega- tion was bowed down, and there was scarcely an eye that was not moist with tears.   It was a model funeral sermon—one of few, simple words,

but every word befitting—and it seemed to me,
a stranger and a spectator, that it was a *perfect*
sermon for the occasion, and that, had he said
one word more or one word less, or had other
words been chosen than those in which he
expressed his few measured and solemn utter-
ances, it would not have been so.

The congregation then sat quietly—so quietly
that you could almost hear your heart beat—for
the space of several minutes, as if to give all an
opportunity to ponder and realize the solemn
truth the good Deacon had uttered. A short
prayer was made by another father of the
church; then a closing hymn was sung by the
congregation, less solemn than the first, with
more of heaven in it than the grave; and then
the Deacon, raising his right hand upwards, pro-
nounced this benediction: " May the Almighty
God of the Universe bless, protect and guide us
all while we live, and at death take us to himself in the realms of unending happiness." And

the response, hearty and distinct, came up from all over the house, " Amen !"

The services were ended—the people slowly moved out of the church, and, after lingering awhile, conversing together, in little groups, in the church-yard and on the roadside, dispersed, each to his own home.   Never in all my life had I attended a religious service which affected me more, or impressed itself more deeply upon my memory, than the brief, appropriate, sincere tribute paid by his surviving neighbors to a dead friend in that little country church on the hill. I have listened to the masterly eloquence of the greatest preachers, but, to my mind, as I recall them now, their sermons were tame and power-less as compared to the brief, simple, eloquent funeral sermon of good Deacon Jones, who, as he afterwards informed me, was but a " plain, common man," without any opportunities for education, much less for the cultivation of the oratorical art, in his early years.

And—need I say it ?—the effect of that funeral

incident, with the Deacon's judicious, well-timed and impressive words there spoken, and with what, sitting beside Mary Jones during the services, I observed of her deep-hearted sympathy with her father and with the solemnity of the occasion—she wept and sighed as though the deceased had been her nearest, dearest friend—was to fan the already burning flame of my affections toward that young lady : and when we arose from our seats, and were advancing towards the door in the aisle, I took her hand gently into mine, and whispered : " Your father is a saint, Miss Jones—and—and—for his sake, as well as for your own, I—I—I—" but I did not finish my intended remark, owing to the coming up of Mr. Bingle, who said Laura was waiting at the church door to speak with me. It was just as well, I suppose—just as well, that I did not, there and then, say to Mary Jones what I wished. But while I was whispering to her she pressed my hand, and that was enough.

CROSS-PURPOSES.

CHAPTER XII.

CROSS-PURPOSES.

COMING out of the little church on the hill, I met Laura at the door, and she requested me to accompany her to her uncle's and spend the remainder of the day, saying she had a matter of great moment to speak to me about, alone. It was quickly arranged. Laura and Mary Jones arranged it in a twinkling. Trust the ladies when it comes to arranging matters. My friend Joe was to accompany Deacon Jones and Mary to their home, and I was to accompany Laura and her uncle to theirs; and in the evening Joe and Mary were to come over to Laura and her uncle's, and thence we could go to our hotel at the station in the evening, as we desired, for an early start in

the train for Westerly next morning. That is
the way they arranged it, and of course Joe and
I had to submit and acquiesce. Laura and
Mary both insisted, and when a lady insists, all
that a gallant young gentleman can do is to bow
his head and give his assent.

So that is the way it was. Joe went home
with Mary and her father, while I went home
with Laura and her uncle. I must confess to
you that the arrangement did not meet with my
cordial concurrence; I did not like the idea of
Joe Startling, chum and friend of mine though
he was, spending an entire afternoon alone with
angelic Mary Jones, whom I admired, on seeing
her on this occasion, more than ever before, and
the sincere respect and veneration with which I
became inspired for her saintly father, after that
impressive service in the church, had the effect
of stimulating the esteem—shall I call it love?—
with which I had from the very first become
inspired regarding her. But the ladies them-

selves had arranged the programme, and submission was a necessity of the hour.

Dinner at noon—a chat with the family in the parlor—a stroll through the garden and the lawn with Laura—tea in the evening, and then a moonlight walk. These were the incidents of my Sunday visit at Mr. Bingle's. But this is a mere outline. What was said between Laura and I during that eventful afternoon and evening would fill volumes. I can report for the reader's edification only one bit of the conversation, which occurred after leaving the parlor for a stroll in the garden:

"What is it, Laura, that you are so anxious to tell me — that 'important matter' you hinted at?"

"Well," she replied, "before I tell you, I wish to know what really are the personal relations between you and my good cousin Frances Wilkins."

"The relations between us, as you know," I

9

said, "have always been very friendly; I esteem Frances very much."

"But you don't really *love* her, do you, Sam?"

"I cannot honestly say that I do not," was my frank reply. "But why do you ask me these questions? What has Frances to do with the important matter you have to tell me?"

"Only this, Sam," she said, pressing my arm impulsively, "that Frances Wilkins has promised to marry another man."

"What! Mr. Gentry?"

"Yes, Mr. Gentry!"

"How do you learn this?"

"I received a letter this very morning from Frances herself, in which she tells me so—and, what is more, Sam, there is a very mysterious expression in her letter, which annoys me, as I think it will you, but you may know its significance better than I do, and therefore I tell you of it. The expression is this," and she produced the letter, and pointed out to me these words: "And now, Laura, I wish you joy of

Sam Traverse—he is yours without any further rivalry from me. I have been apprised of the loving time he and you had together lately at uncle Bingle's."

I was astonished at first—then vexed; and I observed that Laura watched me very closely— studied my face as if to read therein the revelation of a mystery.

"Laura," I said, after a brief pause, in order to compose my confused senses, "I am surprised at this, and yet am not surprised when I come to think of some recent incidents at your aunt Wilkins' house." And then I gave her a history of Mr. Gentry's visit; of Frances' exhibition of jealousy when I told her of my professional visit to Deacon Jones', which so accidentally resulted in my meeting her (Laura,) at her uncle's, and of the subsequent conversation at the tea-table, in which Frances and her mother complimented Mr. Gentry. "It is well as it is, Laura. Frances and I may have thought much of each other, as you and I did when you were one of our family; but no confessions of love have ever been exchanged between us, and I do not see, under the circumstances, why she should not love and marry another man."

"I will tell you now, Sam," Laura said, "and tell you frankly, that Frances and I have often had little contests and fits of jealousy in reference to yourself, as to which of us you thought most of. You now tell me that no confessions of love have ever passed between you and her;— such confessions have passed between you and me, though—and—and," she hesitated, and then asked, "Now tell me, honest and true, you *meant* it, did you not, Sam?"

And she pressed the arm which she held very closely and looked up into my face very earnestly.

"Laura, what I have said to you I *mean* with all my heart; and I believe—yes, I know—*you* mean it, too."

Much more was said—words of earnest sentiment—words too sacred to be repeated here.

The afternoon passed off pleasantly at Mr. Bingle's—so did the evening in the moonlight. At the same time I could not help wondering to myself, occasionally, what Joe and Mary were saying and doing over at Deacon Jones' together.

The evening hours were speeding their course into the night, when, while sitting on the veranda, Laura and I heard voices, and saw two forms approaching in the pathway through an adjoining field, by the moonlight. The voices and the forms were those of Joe and Mary. They joined us, but the hour was so late that we could not tarry much longer. Mary was to spend the night with Laura, and we two beaux bade them good night, and directed our steps toward our hotel at the station.

A FRIEND'S MYSTERY.

CHAPTER XIII.

"SAM," said Joe, while we were leisurely walking down the highway toward the hotel, after leaving the ladies at Mr. Bingle's veranda, "that Miss Mary Jones is a perfect treasure—as beautiful as could be, and as bright and lovely as she is beautiful."

"I am glad you agree with me in this respect," I said; "but how about Laura?—what think you of her?"

"There is really but little choice between the two," he said, hesitatingly; "both are charming ladies, worthy of the love of the best men that ever breathed. Laura would make you a good wife, Sam—I know that, and I could very readily perceive that she adores you. As regards Mary

Jones, I must acknowledge to you that she is the first young woman that I have ever met that I could fall in love with, completely and over-whelmingly. She is a most delightful young lady."

"Well," I said, "I am glad to see you so enthusiastic. You are in raptures over Mary, and yet suggest that Laura would make me a good wife. Why might not Mary make a better?"

"I could tell you, Sam, but you must excuse me now. You marry Laura first, then I will tell you."

"More mystery!" I exclaimed.

"You invited me down here to help you come to a decision as between these two ladies. All I can say, as the result of what I have seen and know of them now, is, marry Laura Ferris. You will never regret it—I'm sure of that."

"You may be right—you may be right," I said, musingly; "but I would like to know why you advise me thus."

"Well," he replied, "in the first place, you know her well, and know that she is an excellent lady; in the next place, she knows you well, and loves you; and, in the last place, you are over head and ears in love with her."

This ended our conversation on that topic for that night. Reaching the hotel at the station, we retired, rising early next morning, and, taking the first train, were speedily transported back to Westerly.

The mystery involved in Joe's remark — "marry Laura first, then I will tell you" — bothered me from the moment he uttered it. The same indescribable emotion came over me that I experienced when Mrs. Wilkins and Frances, at the breakfast table, praised Mr. Gentry to me. It was jealousy. I at once suspected that it was as I had feared it would be that that Sunday afternoon and evening alone with the pretty Mary Jones would result in Joe's falling in love with her and she with him. The thought at first troubled me—and it continued to trouble me

even after I had reached my office and tried to
dispose of some professional business that was
awaiting my attention. Somehow, while I was
drawing up a brief for a client, in a pending suit,
the name of Mary Jones and the pretty face of
Mary Jones would, in spite of me, come flitting
like a thing of beauty across my mind, and,
involuntarily, I would shake my head and pro-
test myself a silly fool. And then, looking out
at my window, I chanced to see, passing by on
the street, a short, sprightly lass, with auburn
hair, reminding me, with a thrill of joyousness,
of Laura Ferris—vivacious, affectionate, confiding creature—and then, pacing the office floor, I
finally declared to myself that Joe was right—
his advice was good; I felt that I indeed loved
Laura, that she indeed loved me, and that she
would indeed be a good wife. "Why then
bother my head further about Mary Jones or
Frances Wilkins, or anybody else?"

I wonder—I wondered then, and have a thousand times wondered since—whether young men

are, as a rule, so unstable of mind, so irresolute
of purpose, as regards the question of the be-
stowal of their affections and the choice of a
wife, as I was.   After these many years of
experience and observation in the world and its
society, I have never found exactly such a case
as mine—such an instance of uncertainty, inde-
cision and suspense; and yet such cases may be
as plenty as there are young men and young
women, for aught I know—it is impossible to
read hearts or to penetrate the secrets of man's
inmost nature.   But I hope men are not, as a
rule, bothered and self-tormented as I was in
this regard; if they are, I pity them; they are
deserving of compassion, for they do not suspect
what fools they are.   Were I, at my present time
of life, to be asked my honest advice by a young
man who was halting between two or three
opinions—or, rather, between two, three or more
female objects of his affectionate contemplation,
I would bluntly tell him: "Interest yourself in
only one at a time, and if you are convinced

that she is the right one, take her, and let that be the end."

Perhaps, however, I am not a good adviser in this matter. Having myself not had the sense to act according to this rule, possibly—I say possibly—I may not have sense enough even now to give safe advice, or any advice, on the subject. But I give it as my candid opinion that if some wise friend had given me some such advice when I first commenced floundering in the midst of my great quandary, it would have served me to good purpose. And yet you are right, sir,—and I will not stop to dispute it— when you say that most young men are queer fellows—that you must let the human nature that is in them work out its own destiny—that, by giving them advice upon such subjects, you are only wasting your precious breath. It might—possibly and perhaps—have proved so in my case. Very likely—very likely.

AN ORDEAL.

CHAPTER XIV.

AN ORDEAL.

ENTERING the drawing-room at Mrs. Wilkins' one evening, many days after the events of the foregoing chapters—the mother and daughter having in the meantime treated me with all the friendly consideration of former times—I soon discovered in their faces and actions that something unusual had occurred— that a cloud had suddenly come athwart their domestic sky. It was soon explained.

"I received a letter from Laura to-day," remarked Frances, addressing me, and then she commenced sobbing, but presently continued, "and she tells me, Sam, that you and she are betrothed."

10

"That is true, Frances," I said—and so it was—Laura and I, by an interchange of letters, had within a few days pledged each other to each other in real earnest—"But why," I asked, "should you feel badly about it?"

"I suppose there is no good reason why I should, Sam," she said, in a voice that trembled with emotion; "but you might at least have intrusted the secret to me, who have so long been as a sister to you. And—and," she sobbed as if her heart would break, "I suppose I ought not to tell you now, but I have loved you, Sam; but it is now too late to talk about that. I feel very, very miserable. Pardon this confession and this exhibition of childishness."

"But I had learned, Frances—and not from yourself, either," I said, "that you are engaged to be married to Mr. Gentry."

"It was Laura who told you that," she said; "in a moment of foolish jealousy I wrote her that, wickedly thinking to annoy both you and her. Mr. Gentry appears to be a fine gentleman, and is a suitor for my hand, but there is no engagement between us, and probably never will be."

"Really, Frances," I said, rising, "I am very sorry that events have taken the turn they have. You and I have been warm friends so long that I grieve to know that I have been the innocent cause of giving you pain. We must and will be friends—yes, sister and brother—hereafter as we have been heretofore. Laura and I are engaged to be married, it is true—and we love each other very truly, you may be assured. The reason I did not apprise you of my intentions and plans was that I supposed it was a fact that you and Mr. Gentry were engaged. You remember how you distrusted me when I returned from my accidental meeting with Laura at Trowbridge, and how you and your mother spoke of Mr. Gentry at the tea-table that evening. That, taken in connection with what you wrote to Laura, decided my course. All I can say now— and I say it from the bottom of my heart—is, that I have always loved you, and am sincerely sorry that I did not know your feelings and the true state of affairs."

I suddenly stopped.   Something seemed to whisper to my soul that I was saying too much and I concluded abruptly.   Heavens! what a fool I am—I thought—ready to fall in love anew with her who was really my first love, after I had pledged myself, heart and hand, to another! I, a lawyer, who is looked to for safe advice by his clients—hoping to be a judge on the bench, sometime, perhaps—have not sufficient power of judgment or decision to know my own mind for a week at a time in a matter so immediately personal 'to myself as that of a preference between women!   What would be the result if I should be called upon to give an opinion or pass judgment upon an intricate question in which the most sacred interests of individuals or communities were involved?   This would be a matter of reason, however, rather than feeling.

But, nevertheless, what a shallow, fickle, capricious fellow I am!

These were the thoughts that passed like electric currents through my mind in that moment while sitting alone in the presence of that majestic, noble young woman—the very ideal of womanly dignity and tenderness—while she, dear soul, sat sobbing and sighing by my side.

"Yes, yes, Sam," she finally said, "we will always be friends, but you know we can never be more than that."

"More than that!" I exclaimed, for I had now recovered myself. "To be true and good friends, Frances, is much—very much, indeed, as this world goes. But, trust me, I will be as good a friend to you as a real brother would be. And I wish you would still, and always, regard me in that light. I ask that, wherever we may be and whatever we may be, you will ever regard me as a real brother—one who feels all the interest in you and for you that a real brother can. I mean this, Frances—I do, indeed."

She thanked me and said, " I know you mean it, Sam—I know you do."

Just then her mother entered the room, much to my relief; for then other matters than those of the heart were the subjects of conversation, and one of the severest ordeals of my life was ended.

A REVELATION.

CHAPTER XV.

SITTING in my office one afternoon, I was gratified at receiving a call from my friend and late client, Deacon Jones, of Trowbridge. I received him cordially, of course.

"I came in specially to see you and consult with you," he said, after being seated, "on a matter of the utmost importance to me, Mr. Traverse, and without taking up any more of your time than is necessary, I will at once make known my business."

"Mr. Jones, I assure you that as much of myself and of my time as you require is not only now, but always, at your service," I remarked.

"I thank you, sir, and appreciate your courtesy. I came to ask you regarding Mr. Startling, your friend—who is he, and what is he?"

"A very fine gentleman, I assure you," I replied; "he was a comrade of mine in college, and is a most honorable and worthy man."

"I am glad to hear you say so," he rejoined; "you know him well, do you?"

"There is no man in the world I know better, and no one in whom I have more confidence. But why do you ask concerning him?"

"I come to you in the strictest privacy, and will tell you the object of my inquiry. He has asked my daughter's hand in marriage, and they have asked my consent to their union. My daughter is a very good girl, has been carefully educated, and has ever been dutiful and precious to us. It is hard for my wife and I to make up our minds that she may marry and leave the home of which she has so long been the light and life. But, I suppose, this must be so sooner or later;" and the old gentleman sighed deeply as he said this. "We cannot in reason expect our children, precious as they are to us, to remain with us always. We must be willing to let them do as we did ourselves—marry and establish homes and families of their own. I am persuaded that Mary is greatly devoted to this young gentleman, and he seems to be a very likely man."

"Have no fear of him," I said, with emphasis; "he will prove a good husband and a dutiful and worthy son-in-law. I know him very well. He is one of the most respected and successful merchants of the city, and is the very model of an honest and trusty gentleman."

The Deacon's face, which had on it an anxious, troubled expression when he first came in, now brightened up, and, taking my hand, he smilingly and earnestly said: "I believe you, and am now a happy man. If, as you say, Mr. Startling is a worthy gentleman, who will love and cherish the dear girl, as a true husband should, and as she deserves, it will all be well,

and her mother and father, to whom she is as
the apple of their eye, will feel that the few
remaining years of their lives will be cheered by
the consciousness of her happiness. Good day,
Mr. Traverse—I thank you very heartily—good
day!" and the old gentleman departed with a
light heart.

I wonder if young beaux generally, when they
sue for the hands and hearts of the daughters of
such parents as Mary Jones had—good people,
who rear their children with care and love them
fondly—have anything like a just appreciation
of the great request they make, and the great
sacrifice they demand of them. I have seen
mothers weep and fathers look sad during the
marriage service that gave their daughters to the
possession of strangers. When I was a very
young man I marvelled at this : not so now, for
I have learned to appreciate their situation, and
understand how like plucking out the heart it is
for fond parents to give up, at the marriage
altar, the daughters of their years of care and

affection. They see their beloved ones embark-
ing upon a sea that is new to them, and upon
which many as dear and precious as they have
found rough sailing, and even fatal shipwreck.
Don't wonder at a parent's anxiety—it is the
most natural thing in the world. And, as I now
look back and recall this confidential interview
with good old Deacon Jones, I honor him for
the anxiety he then exhibited to know who Joe
Startling was, and for the relief and gratification
he manifested when assured that he was a worthy
gentleman.

But these thoughts did not occur to me then.
Another subject of contemplation occupied my
mind after the Deacon's departure. I recalled
that Sunday visit of Joe and myself to the
Joneses and the Bingles, and the misgivings I
then had, in connection with my own purposes,
of the propriety of the arrangement Laura and
Mary made, by which Joe was given the unexpected privilege of spending an afternoon and
evening with the Deacon's charming daughter.

"It turned out just as I apprehended," I mused
to myself, "and now I see that my sudden and
uncomfortable feeling of jealousy, when Joe advised me to marry Laura, and refused to tell me
why he commended her rather than Mary to me,
was not without reason." My suspicion was
now fully confirmed. Well, so it goes; but I
wished them joy—I did, indeed—for I was well
aware that I could not, without joining the
Turks—there were no Mormons then—possess
more than one wife at a time. The fates had
decreed that that one should be Laura, and
surely I should not begrudge my excellent old
chum and friend the possession of Mary. But,
somehow so preposterous is the innate nature
of man—I could not at first, without a real
struggle of contending emotions, reconcile to my
ideas of right and duty the necessity of giving
up all claim to that lovely and beautiful young
woman. Finally, however, after reproaching
myself for my selfishness, unreasonableness and
folly; after reminding myself of the sacredness

of my plighted faith to Laura; after analyzing and weighing my real feelings toward my betrothed, as I had done often before, and satisfying myself of the genuineness of my affection for her; after recalling all the pleasant incidents of my association with her, both at our home at Mrs. Wilkins', and at Mr. Bingle's, and thinking of her many words and acts of love and confidence; after going gravely and thoughtfully through all this process of self-examination and reflection, I reached the conclusion that May Jones belonged as much and as rightfully to Joe Startling as Laura Ferris belonged to Sam Traverse, and that henceforth no woman, be she ever so womanly, no maiden, be she ever so winning, no lady, be she ever so beautiful—not even if she be the very queen of her sex—shall divide with Laura the affection of my heart—I owe it all to her—the dear sister that was, the dear love that is, the loyal and true wife I know very well she would be.

Having finally come to this well-settled conclusion, I gradually dismissed from my mind all thoughts of my old love for the dignified and majestic Frances Wilkins, whom I met daily, and in a very friendly way, at her mother's house, which continued to be my home, and—strange to say—almost forgot the lovely Mary Jones. Laura, whom I visited occasionally, and with whom I corresponded daily, had indeed, and in very truth, become the sole idol of my heart.

So it is that we can govern and subject our emotions and passions and control ourselves, if we do but exercise the will-power that is innate within us, and earnestly follow out the dictates of our reason and our enlightened sense of duty to ourselves and to others. Not that I would have you think that my exclusive devotion to Laura, finally, was a mere matter of will and reason—it was more than that—it was, in addition to these, the prompting of as genuine a love as ever inspired the heart of man. So I thought, and so I felt.

IN THE GREAT CITY.

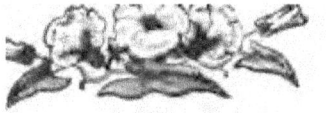

CHAPTER XVI.

IN THE GREAT CITY.

I HAD occasion to go to the great city at the East, on business for a client, in mid-winter. It was a tedious journey, and an unfortunate time to be away from home; snow, cold weather, and a general conspiracy of the atmospheric elements to render human existence miserable anywhere but at home. When coming out of the vestibule of the post-office in the great city, one evening, I saw a tall, handsome gentleman standing near the door as I was about to go out into the street, and, stopping, I tried to think when and where I had seen him before. I knew I had met him somewhere, but could not recall the time and place. Finally, proceeding to the door at which he was standing, intently reading a letter, I passed behind him, and hastily, perhaps impudently, looking over his shoulder upon the written sheet he held in his hand as I was passing out, I instantly recognized the hand-writing, and at once identified the handsome gentleman as Mr. Gentry. It was a mere acci-dent. The letter he was reading—I could have sworn to it, so well I knew the chirography—was from Frances Wilkins.

I did not stop to speak to him, but going into the street, took a stroll through the principal thoroughfare of the city. It was crowded with people—some going to their homes after the day's labor and business—some on their way to places of amusement—others, like myself, strangers, walking the streets merely to pass away time. Presently a party of three gentle-men passed me hurriedly, and I recognized Mr. Gentry as one of them. They were fine looking men, well dressed, with smooth manners, but too careless in their talk to suit my notions of gen-tlemanly propriety.

"Look here, Gent," I heard one of the trio

say, as they were passing me, "why are you so
glum to-night? What's come across you?"

"Nothing of much consequence," he replied;
"only I've just received a long letter from a
sweetheart of mine in the country, and I don't
exactly like the way she writes."

This excited my curiosity at once. I accele-
rated my pace so as to keep near them.

"Love affair, eh?" said one of the other two;
"you ought to have got over that sort of thing
long ago, old fellow. Love? women? Hum-
bug!"

"It does look a little like that," replied Mr.
Gentry; "but if a smart, handsome country lass
gets too sharp for a fellow, it makes him feel
sort o' cheap, you know—and that's what ails
me."

The surging, elbowing, jostling crowd, that
moved, like the currents of two intermingling
but opposing rivers, behind me, before me, and
on either side of me, soon separated the trio of
well-dressed, fast-walking and loud-talking gen-

tlemen from me, and I heard no more of their conversation and lost sight of them.

It was Frances Wilkins that Gentry alluded to, and I wondered what it was that that "country lass" had written to him. "He must be a very smart man," I thought, "if he can get the start of that young lady. Country lass he may deem her, but she has more good sense than the majority of your city flirts—sense enough, I'll warrant, not to be easily captured by any of your flippant city beaux."

This incident revived all my old admiration for Frances. This man Gentry, I thought, has sued for her hand, and sued in vain. He may be a very handsome fellow, very wealthy even, and all that, but Frances Wilkins' heart is not in a condition just now, nor just yet, to be given to a stranger, if to any man. And there, in the midst of that great city, in the midst of that ever-moving, ever-pushing throng of humanity, on that thoroughfare of life and restlessness, my old interest in Frances came back to me. I could not help it—it was a resistless impulse. Mary Jones was nothing to me—and, for the moment, I came near even forgetting my sacred duty to Laura.

"What a simpleton I am!" I exclaimed, aloud, as I entered my room that evening, in the great hotel. "What a fool not to be able to dismiss this feeling, and concentrate, once for all and unchangeably, my love and devotion upon the one to whom my solemn vow has been made."

"And who *is* this man Gentry?" I asked myself, as, thinking over the evening's events, I was vainly trying to compose myself for a good night's sleep, preparatory to my return home next day. "Who is he that thus lightly talks to his fellows in the street about his 'sweetheart in the country?'" I didn't like the flashy looks of his companions, and much less did I like the peculiar manner in which he spoke to them about that "love letter," as he called it.

A DOUBLE WEDDING.

CHAPTER XVII.

A DOUBLE WEDDING.

RETURNING home from the great city, and burying myself in the business of my office, trying hard and successfully to dismiss all thoughts of love and women from my mind, except as to Laura Ferris, I soon succeeded in becoming a complete master of myself. Laura had now come to be indeed the one particular, only object of my affections, and I was a happy man. This feeling and this happiness was increased as, almost daily, I received tender messages and epistles from her.

I met Joe Starling on the street one day and congratulated him upon his triumph in winning Mary Jones. He wanted to know how I had found it out. I did not tell him. "You mysti-

fied me once, my boy," I said, "and now I will
be as mysterious as you were then; but although
I then imagine myself in love with Mary, be
assured, nevertheless, that I was quick to adopt
your advice, to marry Laura. The day is set,
Joe, and I invite you to join a select bridal party
at Mr. Bingle's one month from to-day."

"One month from to-day!" he exclaimed.
"To-day is Tuesday—let me see! Why, Sam,
that is the very day that Mary and I have set for
our marriage."

"Is it possible?" I exclaimed. "Singular
coincidence -isn't it?"

"It is, indeed! but can't we so arrange it as to
attend each other's wedding, Sam?"

And we talked it over further, but failed to see
how the matter could be arranged or rearranged
before consulting the two ladies who were immediately concerned.

I visited Laura a day or two afterwards, and
on announcing to her the fact of Joe's and Mary's
wedding-day being appointed on the same day as

ours, thinking it would be news to her, she let me
into the secret that she and Mary, who, living
neighbors, had always had a good understanding
between themselves, had purposely agreed upon
that day, thinking to surprise their prospective
husbands. And she informed me, furthermore,
that it had been arranged between them that
both parties should be married at the same hour
in the little church on the hill, by the same.
clergyman.

As I had occasion to remark before, trust the
ladies for arranging things. Their ingenuity for
arranging things is only equaled by their intuitive
appreciation of the fitness of things.

Of course, the very next time that Joe saw
Mary, she likewise disclosed to him the secret of
the prearranged double-wedding day—and so it
was well understood by both couples and their
families, and by Mrs. Wilkins and her daughter
Frances, and, indeed, the entire communities
both of Westerly and Trowbridge soon knew of
it. How a secret, once revealed, flies and

becomes a notoriety — especially when such matters as marriage engagements and bridal-days are involved therein.

The month soon passed. The double-wedding took place in the little church on the hill. It was a joyous occasion, of course—very joyous and very delightful. A wedding in the country is always a marked event. There is one such only at great intervals, and then old and young, as if it were a matter of personal duty, take a part in it, directly or indirectly. ·The little church was filled. The congratulations were many and hearty. Good old Deacon Jones and dear old Mrs. Deacon Jones, both as sedate as Quakers when the ceremonies were in progress, became as cheerful and happy after the solemn rites had been performed as the gay-hearted children who lingered around the church porch, and Mr. Bingle and the feeble Mrs. Summerfield, Laura's venerable grandmother, fairly danced for joy when congratulating the newly-married pairs.

"God bless ye, dear children," said the aged grandmother, "God bless ye, and give ye long, happy and prosperous lives, and He surely will, if ye be but true to Him, to yourselves and to each other. Oh, beautiful spectacle!—one to make the very angels of heaven smile—to see four such handsome, likely and loving young people as ye are, starting out together on a career of blessedness! Bless ye, dear children, bless ye!"

The old lady's face shone like that of a sainted patriarch while she spoke, and the earnest kisses she pressed upon our cheeks seemed like sealing for Heaven's ratification her invocation for a blessing upon us.

And there were Mrs. Wilkins and Frances, the noble young woman! They, too, were warm in their congratulations, and the latter, after kissing Laura, kissed my cheek, and whispered, "Oh, Sam! be happy, but never forget me!" "Never, Frances," I whispered in reply, "never while I have life." And she was happy—I could see it in her large, dark eyes, and a smile crept over her queenly face like a ray of sunshine. And we were all happy together there, in that sacred little church on the hill—very happy, very joyous—very, very indeed.

A wedding tour to the West, and, after a month's absence, our return to Westerly, and then a settling down into quiet homes. Deacon Jones purchased a grand house for his Mary and her husband; and Laura's grandmother—dear old soul—gave my wife a title-deed to a fine house in the city—"the old homestead," she said, "in which I lived when I was a bride, and in which Laura's mother was born." And our happiness did not end with the close of our honeymoon—oh, no—it was as continuous as the light of the sun.

With our final settling down in a home of our own, the ardor of our mutual affections became intensified, and our married life became literally a reciprocity of idolatry, and all went well. In my profession I began to prosper rapidly, and the law office of Samuel Traverse gradually became one of the, chief ones in the city. Friends, clients and business increased daily, and all went well.

All went well, too, with Joe and Mary, who were very happy—very devoted—very blessed.

12

THE FAIR WEEK.

CHAPTER XVIII.

THERE was a great fair week in Westerly in the autumn—one of those annual assemblages of the people of a wide region of country to see the gathering together of the sample products of stable, soil, shop, factory and studio, for which this favored part of the world is noted. It was a great week. The exhibition was magnificent in everything almost that the labor, skill and ingenuity of man could produce. It was a vast show of animals, machinery, vegetable and floral wonders, farm products, fruits, woman's handiwork, the artist's genius and the artisan's skill. The city was alive with people—country people and village people, young and old. They came in from the distance of an hundred miles, in carriages, on horseback and on foot. The country highways were animate with comers and goers. It was a great week. The hotels and the boarding-houses of the city were crowded to the utmost capacity of their accommodations, and every private house in the town had its guests. The stores and the shops swarmed with people, and the streets were filled with flowing and inter-mingling currents of humanity. It was a grand gala-week. The extensive fair grounds were literally covered with human beings, and the great exhibition halls swarmed like vast bee-hives. It was a glorious week for Westerly. The weather was as pleasant and balmy as that of an Italian May, and the sky as bright as that of a tropical summer. A great week it was for the country and the town—a holiday-week—a week of amuse-ment and festivity. The men and the women, old and young—the children, and all—made it a week of unusual pleasure and gayety.

Mr. and Mrs. Deacon Jones came up from Trowbridge and spent the week with Joe and

Mary, and Mr. Bingle and grandmother Summer-field came up and spent the week with Laura and I. And, one day, while pushing our way through the multitude at the fair grounds, Laura and I and Joe and Mary and the rest of us, all unex-pectedly came upon Mrs. Wilkins and Frances, under the gentlemanly escort of Mr. Gentry. They were enjoying the sights, and, meeting us, stopped just long enough to exchange salutations, and were soon lost in the throng again.

"That man Gentry I don't like," I remarked to Joe. "I cannot tell why, but I am suspicious of that fellow, and I don't like to see him coming to Mrs. Wilkins' house so often."

Joe said nothing. It was not the time nor place to discuss people's individual characters. We ourselves, in such a vast crowd as was there assembled, felt like mere drops in an ocean. We were very small parts of the big mass. Mr. Gentry was as large and as small as every other one of the crowd, no more and no less, but I could not help feeling troubled about Frances on his account. I had a premonition that his presence here in Westerly would eventually cause trouble. In other words, I was fearful that he would gain the heart of Frances Wilkins, and after what I had seen of him and heard him say in the crowded thoroughfare of the great city, I became distrustful of him. I feared that he was not a good man—not the man for the noble Frances Wilkins. I mentioned my misgivings to Laura that day. "Never mind, Sam," she said "Frances is in no danger of capture by a stranger. She will never leap in the dark. Set your mind at rest in that regard."

"But what is the fellow doing here at this time? Why does he visit at Mrs. Wilkins' so often, unless he meets with encouragement?"

Laura did not know, but still thought there was no danger—that Frances knew what she was about, and that Mr. Gentry must prove up his credentials very satisfactorily before she could be induced to give herself to him.

The fair week closed. Our visitors departed.

The fair grounds and the exhibition halls were deserted. The streets of the city resumed their ordinary, common-place aspect. But it had been a great week for Westerly, and for all the country round about.

A DEATH-BED REQUEST

CHAPTER XIX.

A DEATH-BED REQUEST.

THE sky is bright and the world beautiful to-day; to-morrow come clouds and gloom.

There is no pain like that of the sympathy and anxiety of the loving heart when the object of its devotion lies prostrate, helpless and suffering on a bed of illness—when neither physician can afford relief nor care or tenderness bring comfort or hope—when death threatens life, and your very soul trembles in apprehension of the approaching crisis.

The second anniversary of our marriage had scarcely passed, when Laura—my wife, my idol— was attacked by a burning, consuming, merciless fever. Day after day, night after night, for many

weary, troublous, anxious weeks, we watched by
her bedside, helpless for her relief. She was
fading away. The cheek that had been so full
and fresh, was now sunken and pale; the deep
blue eye that had shone with love and life, was
now dull and fireless; the form that had been so
full of life and buoyancy, was now a mere skele-
ton—thin, and as helpless as that of an infant.

"What think you now, doctor?" I asked of the
physician one morning, after a sleepless, restless,
anxious night.

"She is dying, sir—she is dying," he said,
solemnly.

And it was so. The idol of my soul was being
snatched from me, and I was a gloomy, wretched
man.

"Samuel," she said, in a feeble whisper, "I
am going—oh, it is so hard to leave you; but
God's will be done—God's will be done. He
has always been good to us, and always will be."
She paused for breath, and then, pressing my
hand with a final pressure—it was the last time,

and I thought my heart would break—she said, "Samuel, my love, when I am gone, seek another wife—one who will be true to you and worthy of you. Marry Frances, Samuel—she loves you, and will be as true to you as I have been. Marry Frances, Samuel, and God bless you!"

These were her last words. She folded her snow-white hands over her breast, closed her eyes, and it was all over. The house that had but a few weeks before been the home of love and joy and promise, was now a house of gloom and grief and mourning. Its very soul had gone out—its presiding deity had been snatched away ruthlessly, cruelly.

"I am alone in the world once more—all, all alone;" thus I spake inconsolably to myself, on the desolate evening of that day on which we consigned her precious form to its last resting-place in the cold, damp earth. "All, all alone! Oh, that I, too, could die, and thus end this woe and dreariness of soul!"

It was many weeks before I could recover from

the cruel blow that had fallen upon me. My grief was profound and depressing, and I wandered about, in my office, in the street, in my desolate home, a gloomy, wretched man, who felt that he had now nothing to live for—that he had lost everything worth having in this world, and that death was preferable to life.

THE OLD LOVE.

CHAPTER XX.

THE OLD LOVE.

BUT no man—and no woman, either—can nurse a great sorrow for a long time and live in sanity. Mine gradually became less a burden; by immersing myself in the business of my profession, I eventually conquered myself, and ceased to grieve like one who had lost all.

Joe Startling was in my office one afternoon, trying, as he had so often tried before, to console and cheer me. It was several months after Laura's death.

"I this morning saw Mr. Gentry," he said, "coming out of Mrs. Wilkins' house. Is he still a suitor for Frances' hand?"

Somehow this announcement awoke me as if from a deep sleep.

"Mr. Gentry? Frances?" I said; "that cannot be, I think. I do not believe she would ever marry him. Do you know him, Joe?"

"I have inquired, and now know who he is, but have no personal acquaintance with him," said he; "he is not a man for Frances Wilkins to marry that I know. He is a—a—gambler— · a professional sporting man—an adventurer."

"You astonish me!" I exclaimed. "It cannot be that Mrs. Wilkins and her daughter are aware of his character. They must be informed."

And I instantly seized my hat, and leaving Joe at the first street corner, hurried to Mrs. Wilkins'. I found mother and daughter at home. After preliminary conversation, I sought an opportunity to allude to Mr. Gentry.

"I understand," I finally said, "that Mr. Gentry is in town to-day."

"Yes," said Mrs. Wilkins, rising, "he called here this morning—it was his first visit for several weeks."

The mother then left the room, and Frances and I were alone—alone for the first time since the night of that ordeal when she had first learned that Laura and I were engaged to be married.

"Frances," said I, "on the day when Laura and I were married, in the little church on the hill, in Trowbridge, you and I exchanged whispered words—do you remember them?"

"I do, indeed, and will never forget them. I then asked you never to forget me, and I do not know what spirit of good or evil impelled me to do so—it was hardly the proper thing to do under the peculiar circumstances. And I remember your answer—that you never would forget me while you had life; that answer made me very happy, Samuel—why, I cannot tell."

"You remember, too," I said, "the night when, in this very room, you upbraided me, with tears, for having engaged myself to your cousin Laura without intrusting the secret to you, who had always been a sister to me."

"I remember it well—very well; and I remember equally well what you then said to me—
that you would always be as a brother to me—a
true friend, wherever or whatever we may be?"

"I am glad you remember these circumstances and assurances so well, Frances, because
I have come now to demonstrate my brotherly
and friendly interest in you. Pardon me if I ask
you a delicate question. Do you love this man
Gentry? Is there anything more than ordinary
friendship between you?"

"He appears to be a very fine and accomplished gentleman," she replied, "but I have
given him no encouragement, and I do not wish
to marry. I once had such a thought, several
years ago, but it was a girlish whim, and I then
dismissed it, and have never since then had
occasion to change my resolution. But why do
you ask me concerning Mr. Gentry?"

"Because I have this day learned who and
what he is, and have deemed it my duty to tell
you. He is a professional gambler, Frances,

and I am sure you would have nothing more to do with him if you were aware of the fact."

"Are you sure that that is his business?" she asked, in surprise, her face becoming flushed.

I gave her my authority, and knowing that Joe Startling would not repeat such a statement unadvisedly, she at once conceded the probability of its truth, and thanked me for the warning, assuring me again, however, that there was nothing serious between her and Gentry, and that nothing was further from her thoughts than that of being led captive by him. "There is only one man in the world that I have seen or known," she then concluded, "that I have ever dreamed of loving, but, as I said before, it was, perhaps, a girlish whim, merely, and I dismissed it as soon as I discovered my folly."

As she said this, she turned her head away, but I could see a troubled look—a half-sad, half-painful expression—on her face. A brief silence followed, and as I sat silently admiring that womanly figure, and studying the outlines of that queenly face—a face that a painter or a sculptor would adopt as a model of perfection—a face that could be all sunshine at one moment, and all dignified repose the next—whose formation was like that of a sculptured Cleopatra or a Venus—it occurred to me suddenly, as if a flash of light had sent the thought into my soul, that, possibly, her old love for me was still alive, and that this is what she meant by the "girlish whim" of former years to which she mysteriously referred.

"Tell me, Frances," I said, persuasively, "who was the man you refer to, whom you once thought of as a lover?"

"That is a secret I can never disclose to you, Samuel; it is the only secret I can never tell you."

"Well, Frances," I said, drawing my chair near her's, and taking her hand, "there is one secret that I have now kept concealed in my own bosom for months, which I could not and never will tell to any living soul except yourself."

And then I repeated to her these dying words of my wife: "Marry Frances—she loves you, and will be as true a wife to you as I have been."

"Oh, Samuel!" she exclaimed, with emotion, her whole face suddenly lighting up, "Laura knew how I"—but she abruptly stopped there.

"Well, what did Laura know?"

"I was on the point of revealing to you the very secret that I a moment ago refused to tell you. First, Samuel, let me ask you a question: Have you ever loved me could you, or do you now love me? Tell me honestly, frankly."

"Frances," I said, conscious that now candor and plain speech were in order, "at the time when Laura and I became engaged to be married, I was in a painful quandary as to which of you I loved the more, and to this day I cannot decide which of you I then did love the best; but I have often thought, and I still think, that it is more than probable that, but for my mistaken supposition that you were engaged to Mr.

Gentry, I would have asked you to become my wife. I have loved Laura truly—her death seemed to me the end of everything—and even now, when I permit myself to think of her, and of how precious she was to me, I become sad and wretched under the consciousness of my great loss. You will not wonder at this, for you know how true a wife she was to me."

"No, Samuel, I honor your feelings in this respect," she said.

"Well," I continued, "you ask me whether I could or do love you now, Frances. In answer to that, I here and now offer you my hand, feeling and knowing that my other love—she who has been so much and so dear to me—would, if she could witness this scene, rejoice and bless us."

"You are sincere, Sam—I see and know and feel that you are," she said, "and now I am really, really happy—now I have the wish of my soul—I have *you*, dear, good, brotherly Sam—I have you, whom I have loved so long and yet so silently. I will now finish what I had intended to say—that Laura knew how I loved you—how eagerly I hoped, in that test scene which she and I arranged at mother's, years ago—you remember it when we resorted to what we deemed a shrewd device to ascertain which of us two you loved best—you would in some way, by word or act, indicate your preference for me. It was a girlish affair on our part, I now freely confess ; but when you refused to decide, and when afterwards I learned of your visiting Laura at her uncle's, I despaired, and have been the most wretched creature ever since. It is all over now, and, Samuel, be assured that Laura's dying words will prove to have been the truest words that human lips have ever uttered. I do love you, and I know I will be a true wife to you. Oh, Samuel! God is good, and He orders the affairs of His creatures mysteriously, but for the best at last."

It was a rapturous outburst of long pent-up feeling. Her every word, her every tone of utterance, the earnest expression of her big, dark eyes, the warm pressure of her hands and arms, convinced me, beyond the possibility of doubting, that Frances Wilkins loved me—and instantly, as if the stone of the sepulchre of my heart's buried affections had been suddenly rolled away from the closed door, the old, old feeling came back to me—the old, old love—my first love—and once again life and love were mine.

It is difficult to reconcile these changes of the emotions and affections of the human heart. Only a few months ago—months of anguish and dreariness of soul—months of grieving and sorrowing—I longed to go down into the grave in which my precious Laura lay buried, and lie by her side in death; while now life had a new and intensified charm for me. Those last words of the dear, dying wife, which at the moment of their utterance I regarded as not possible of fulfillment, proved to be the talismanic sign which resurrected and reinspired a broken heart, and restored the manhood of my nature from its lost estate.

It was only a few months subsequently when there was another wedding, at which Mr. and Mrs. Joe Startling, Mr. and Mrs. Deacon Jones, Mr. Bingle, the saintly old grandmother, Mrs. Wilkins and her stately daughter, my love and my bride, were present. And my love and my bride was then and there—not in the little country church on the hill, but in the mansion of Samuel Traverse, in Westerly—made the wife of Samuel Traverse aforesaid, in form and manner as in such cases made and provided by law. Again there were congratulations, hearty and earnest. The good old grandmother again invoked heaven's blessings, and sealed them with a kiss. Mr. and Mrs. Deacon Jones again were joyful of heart. Mr. Bingle, worldly man as he was, when he pressed my hand, remarked : " Lawyer Sam, Laura was a jewel, and now you have another treasure ; bless you, my boy, but don't forget to come out to Trowbridge occa-

sionally." And then Joe and Mary—Mr. and
Mrs. Startling—my ever-faithful old chum, with
one of my old loves clinging closely to his
arm—came up to Frances and I, and after wishing us joy, Joe was about to say something
which Mary commanded him peremptorily not
to, and he didn't; but afterwards he did. "I'm
bound to say it," he exclaimed, "and now, dear,
don't be foolish—I *will*, and here goes. Sam,
next time you go a courting in the country, don't
take with you a better looking fellow than you
are yourself—it isn't safe." Mary blushed—
Frances looked interrogatively—and the good
old Deacon Jones, who stood near by and heard
what was said, remarked: "You trust Lawyer
Sam. He knows what he's about all the time."

THE CONCLUSION.

CHAPTER XXI.

THE CONCLUSION.

ONCE again there was a settling down into the quiet of domestic comfort. Once again the sun of hope and promise shone bright in the sky. Once again I was one of the happiest men in the world.

My law business continued to flourish amazingly. My friends soon became as numerous as the inhabitants of Westerly and the region round about. My house was the center of social enjoyment, and my stately, dark-haired, dark-eyed, noble-faced, great-souled wife was beloved by everybody and worshiped by her husband.

All this was long ago. We have grown old since then, but are happy still.

Have you, in your wanderings in the region

14

about Westerly, within the past decade, heard of
old Judge Traverse? Yes, sir, *old* Judge Traverse, whose opinion in matters of the law, there-
abouts, is equal to the " so says the gospel " in
matters of religion? That old fellow is me—
Sam Traverse—lawyer that was, Judge of the
Circuit Court that is, and if you should ever
chance to come around there again, drop into
the old Judge's little paradise of a home, see the
now gray-haired but still beautiful Frances, and
share with us the kindly gifts that a good Provi-
dence has bestowed upon us. And, as like as
not, you will, of a pleasant afternoon or evening,
find there Mr. and Mrs. Joe Startling, as devoted
to each other as of yore. They are also among
the old folks now, and we are near neighbors,
and all very good people, who are always glad to
see their friends. If you desire, on some Saturday afternoon, we—Joe and Mrs. Joe, and Sam
Mrs. Sam—will make up a gay little party for
you, and take the cars for Trowbridge Station—
stop at the hotel there over night—go and see

where good old Deacon Jones used to live—but he's been dead these thirty years, and his sacred dust lies in the grave-yard back of the little church on the hill. Near the graves of the Deacon and his good wife, you will also see tombstones marked with the names of Laura's sainted old grandmother and her daughter, Laura's mother, and her son-in-law, Mr. Bingle. The old churchyard is full of graves—the dead there elbow each other as the living do in the crowded town. And we will, if you choose, attend service in that little church on the hill, and mingle with the simple country folks we will find there the men and the women who, when, nearly forty years ago, that eventful double wedding took place there, were the little boys and girls who played around the church porch. The old folks of that time are all gone—all gone; and even many of the young folks of that time are gone—scattered world-wide, and some of them resting forever under the sod which hides the dead from the living.

But Frances and I are happy old folks—this I wish to impress upon your mind—we are happy, very happy— have always been so—have always been true and devoted lovers—always—and as the green leaf has gradually but surely assumed a sear and yellow hue, our mated hearts have become more and more one and the same in sympathy and in all things.

"And what became of Mr. Gentry?" I think I hear you inquire. He died many years ago, before those black locks or that dark beard of his had grown gray—a convict in Sing Sing. Forgery was the accusation. He sent for me to defend him at his trial, but it was a hopeless case. "Guilty," was the verdict of the jury, and that was the last of a very handsome but a very useless man. He died in prison, after having served a dozen years of his term of twenty. "God be praised!" were among the last words of old Mrs. Wilkins, my motherly mother-in-law, when, thirty odd years ago, she gave her dying blessing to her daughter; "God be praised,

Frances, that you never married that Mr. Gentry it would have been your ruin." The old lady has a monument over her resting-place—the last tribute of her daughter and her daughter's husband, and the inscription reads thus: "Our Mother—Gone to her God." And near her tomb, in an old church-yard at Westerly, there is another monument, and the inscription upon it reads: "LAURA—GONE TO HEAVEN. SHE WITHERED AND DIED, AS DO THE FLOWERS OF THE SPRING—TOO SOON; BUT GOD'S WILL BE DONE."

Frances and I were walking in our garden last June, she leaning upon my arm, and I leaning upon my friendly staff, and when we came to a certain row of elms skirting the lawn, she said: "Sam, look there—our four children, when they were still quite young, planted those four trees, to represent themselves, to see which would do the best and live the longest. I tended and watched those trees when they were small, very tenderly and carefully, as I had those children. Now see—they are all of a size, and equally vigorous, with great, spreading branches, affording a grateful shade for you and I, from the burning sun. A good omen, my dear old man, a good omen for those precious children of ours, now grown to manhood and womanhood."

It is only necessary to remark—excuse an old man's tediousness—that the oldest of those four children is thirty-six and the youngest twenty-five. They are all married, and when their families gather in the old homestead at Westerly, as they often do, then *do* come there and see us; you will find in our joyous company about a dozen little folks, who call Sam Traverse and his wife grandfather and grandmother.

So goes the world!

FINIS

Milton Keynes UK
Ingram Content Group UK Ltd.
UKHW021336290324
440221UK00003B/55